'Oh!' Penny's gasp sounded almost like a scream. 'Ivy . . .' She pointed, her finger quivering. '*Look!*'

Feeling heavy with dread, Ivy turned . . .

'Oh, no,' she whispered.

The display case she'd closed only a few moments ago hung open . . . and the velvet hanger was empty.

Tessa's priceless pashmina had been stolen!

Sink your fangs into these:

MY SISTER THE VAMPIRE

Switched

Fangtastic!

Revamped!

Vampalicious

Take Two

Love Bites

Lucky Break

Star Style

Twin Spins!

Date with Destiny

Flying Solo

Stake Out!

Double Disaster!

Flipping Out!

Secrets and Spies

MY BROTHER THE WEREWOLF

Cry Wolf!

Puppy Love!

Howl-oween!

Tail Spin

Sienna Mercer

MY SISTER THE VAMPIRE

FASHION FRIGHTMARE!

EGMONT

With special thanks to Stephanie Burgis

For Julia, with love

EGMONT
We bring stories to life

My Sister the Vampire: Fashion Frightmare! first published in
Great Britain 2014 by Egmont UK Limited, The Yellow Building,
1 Nicholas Road, London W11 4AN

Copyright © Working Partners Ltd 2014
Created by Working Partners Limited, London WC1X 9HH

ISBN 978 1 4052 6573 7

1 3 5 7 9 10 8 6 4 2

A CIP catalogue record for this title is available from the British Library

Typeset by Avon DataSet Ltd, Bidford on Avon, Warwickshire B50 4JH
Printed and bound in Great Britain by the CPI Group

54103/1

EGMONT LUCKY COIN

Our story began over a century ago, when seventeen-year-old
Egmont Harald Petersen found a coin in the street.

He was on his way to buy a flyswatter, a small hand-operated
printing machine that he then set up in his tiny apartment.

The coin brought him such good luck that today Egmont has
offices in over 30 countries around the world. And that lucky
coin is still kept at the company's head offices in Denmark.

Chapter One

*D*ING!

The bell over the front door of the Meat and Greet jangled loudly, and Ivy Vega jerked her head up.

Ouch! Pain jolted through her neck. She rubbed at it, sighing, as she looked away from the boy who'd just arrived at the restaurant. He wasn't who she was waiting for.

For the last fifteen minutes, she'd jerked at each ding of the bell. Unfortunately, the Meat and Greet was so crowded today, the bell dinged a *lot*. That meant her neck was starting to feel some serious whiplash!

It's no fun waiting by myself, she thought glumly.

If her best friend, Sophia, had been here, the situation might at least have felt funny . . . but then, if Sophia had been home in Franklin Grove, Ivy wouldn't have had to wait here in the first place. Sophia was away in Tokyo, on a two-week-long vampire student exchange programme. In her place was a Japanese vampire named Reiko, who was due to arrive any moment now.

And I've got to chaperone her – if she ever shows up!

DING!

Ivy's head bounced up again, sending a brand-new stab of pain down her neck. 'Ow!' She clapped one hand to the collar of her jet-black beaded sweater. *This had better be Reiko – because, seriously, I've only got about two more of these reactions left in me before my head just falls off!*

But when Ivy looked closer, she saw not Reiko, but a familiar face: her own! It was her identical, human twin sister, Olivia, wearing a pink cashmere sweater and glittery, embroidered blue jeans. Olivia was beaming as she murmured something into her cell phone. Her smile widened as she caught Ivy's gaze, holding up one finger as she slid into the booth across from her sister.

'I'll see you soon,' she said into the phone. 'I can't wait, either!'

Aha. Ivy grinned. She didn't need her special vampire hearing to know that the voice on the other end was Olivia's movie star boyfriend, Jackson Caulfield.

'So he can come, after all?' Ivy asked, as her twin tucked the phone into her bag.

'Absolutely.' Olivia let out a happy sigh as she sat back in her seat. 'Jackson *will* be in town on Wednesday night – which means that *lots more* news outlets are going to want to cover the event! Isn't that great? So many people are going to find out about Café Creative!'

'Hmm.' Ivy hid a grin as she prepared to tease

her twin. 'Y'know, Franklin Grove isn't *that* big. We probably could have just stood on the roof of the museum with a megaphone, and everyone in town would still have heard about it.'

'True enough.' Olivia laughed. 'But it won't hurt for people *outside* this town to know of it, too. Just think! It could draw creative young people from Lincoln Vale.' She flung out one arm in a sweeping gesture. 'And beyond. After all, any press is good press!'

'*Seriously?*' Ivy stared at her twin, dumbfounded. 'Did you just say what I thought you said?'

'Um . . .?' Olivia raised her eyebrows.

'Pretty soon, I'm going to need a phrasebook to translate all your "Hollywood-ese"!' Ivy told her.

Olivia laughed. 'I'm sure Sophia can help. Fashionista-language can't be all that different, right?' She leaned forwards, nudging aside her beaded purple bag. 'Speaking of whom . . . have you heard anything from her yet?'

Sienna Mercer 🦇

Ivy shrugged. 'Just a one-line email. She said she was pretty jet-lagged, but that Tokyo looked dead cool from the inside of her taxi.'

'Finally!' A stressed-looking waitress hurried towards their table, already scooping out a notepad and pen from her apron. 'I take it you're ready to order now?'

Uh-oh. Ivy winced. It was the most crowded time of day at the Meat and Greet, and she'd already taken up a table for nearly twenty minutes without ordering anything. The waitress had to be ready to tear her own hair out.

Ivy gave a weak smile. 'We're, um, still waiting for one more person, actually.'

The waitress stared at her. 'How much longer do you think they'll be?'

Ivy shook her head helplessly. 'She should have been here twenty minutes ago.'

The waitress's face pinkened. She opened her mouth as if to say something – and since she had the same look on her face that their teacher Mr Russell got whenever he spotted a skateboard inside their school, Ivy was pretty sure whatever she said next would be scathing.

Olivia said hastily, 'I'd love a diet soda, please.'

'Hmmph!' The waitress swung around and stalked away . . . without writing the order down on her notepad.

Olivia sighed. 'I don't think I'm going to get that.'

Ivy slumped in her seat. 'I can't believe how late Reiko is!'

Olivia gave her a sympathetic smile. 'Maybe she has a good excuse?'

'Maybe.' Ivy shook her head. 'I wonder what she's going to be like, though. I've never met a Japanese vamp before – I've heard they're really traditional and strict.'

'Ooohhh.' Olivia's eyes glazed over. 'Do you think she gets to wear kimonos?'

Ivy blinked at her sister. 'Are you fantasising about her *clothing*, now?'

'Why not?' Olivia's lips stretched into a dreamy smile. 'Do you remember that black kimono you wore before the ball last year? It looked so good with your pale complexion.'

'Did I also "look good" on the way home, when I tripped over it and fell flat on my face?' Ivy snorted. 'I have no idea how anyone manages to walk in those things for more than twenty minutes!'

'Well, growing up wearing them probably helps,' Olivia said. 'It must teach grace and poise, balance and posture. Or, in other words . . .' her gaze narrowed '. . . all the things *you're* going to need on Wednesday, at the opening of Café Creative!'

'Aaagh!' Ivy groaned. Her dad and stepmom, Lillian, were opening the converted south wing of the museum with an event showcasing local

7

creative talent. The showpiece was going to be a fashion show put on by Amelia Thompson and Penny Taylor, two students at Franklin Grove High. Somehow, Ivy had agreed to take part . . . as a *model*! She shuddered. 'What was I thinking? Me, parading up and down in fashions designed by girls from our school . . . what in the world could *ever* have made me agree to that?'

Olivia giggled. 'You know the answer already. Lillian's been working on this for weeks – and she has us *both* wrapped around her fingers.'

'Um . . . *huh*?' Ivy pointed one accusing finger straight at her twin. 'I remember the moment Lillian first asked us – you, Olivia Abbott, needed *no* convincing.'

'Of course I didn't. It'll be fun!' Olivia shrugged, smiling irrepressibly. 'Can you imagine what the designs will be like? Penny's half of the show is going to be all bright and bunny-tastic, while Amelia's all about "classy goth". They're going to complement each other perfectly! Plus . . .'

She leaned over the brightly coloured table, dropping her voice to a low whisper. 'Rumour has it they've also worked together on a *hybrid* of both their styles. A joint outfit to be their big finish and close the show. I can't wait!' Letting out a little squeal, Olivia bounced in her seat. 'I can't even *imagine* what such a dress will look like!'

Ivy scowled. 'I suppose it's good at least one of us is excited.' It wasn't often she wished that movie vampire rules were true but, right now, she'd give anything not to be able to show up in photographs. Then, no one would *ever* ask her to stroll up and down a catwalk!

Unfortunately, real vampires showed up perfectly well in photos – and in mirrors, too. The only thing that bunny screenwriters got correct was how much they hated garlic. And Ivy was considering eating some just to get out of this fashion show!

DING!

Ivy looked up sharply. Pain sparked down her neck, but this time she barely noticed. She was in too much shock.

The girl at the door had to be Reiko . . . and she was not what Ivy had been expecting *at all*!

Olivia turned around to follow Ivy's gaze. 'No kimono,' she murmured.

'Nope.' Ivy's eyes widened as she took in the other vamp's bright yellow tank top and neon green athletic shorts. 'And she does not look like she's been raised in a strict community, does she?'

That'll teach me to make assumptions, Ivy thought wryly. Not only was Reiko *not* wearing a kimono, she wasn't even a goth like every single young American vamp Ivy knew.

Instead, she wore clothes that weren't just bright – they were so luminous they could have lit up a pitch-black room! Her shorts even had a logo so big and sporty it made Ivy's fangs itch.

10

But most of all, Ivy couldn't stop staring at Reiko's massive orange backpack.

It had a tennis racquet sticking up out of it.

'Am I dreaming?' Olivia whispered. 'Or am I actually looking at a vampire *tennis player*?'

Ivy could only shake her head wordlessly. 'I've never seen anything like it.'

And that wasn't all. Above the backpack and the tennis racquet, Reiko's long hair – which was a perfectly normal goth shade of purple – bounced in a high, bouncy, cheerleader-style ponytail!

That is so not a vamp look!

'Hey!' Reiko's face lit up in a grin as she saw them. Giving an excited wave, she bounded over to the table in fast, athletic strides. 'You must be Ivy, right? And Olivia! I recognise you both from *Banp* magazine!'

'Did you say *Ban* magazine?' Ivy asked, scooting over on the seat to make room for Reiko and her giant backpack full of sports equipment.

Through the crack in the top of the backpack, she could see tennis balls and even a basketball jostling for space inside.

'No, *Banp*!' Still standing – and bouncing on her toes – Reiko yanked off the backpack and tossed it on to the table.

'Oops!' Olivia jerked out of the way just in time, before the handle of the tennis racquet could slam into her head. She sat back, eyes wide. '*Bamp* magazine?'

'No, no, *Banp*. You know . . .' Reiko slid into the booth beside Ivy, then leaned forwards to whisper, with an infectious grin: 'Japanese for "vamp"!'

'Aha!' Ivy gave a sigh of relief. *Banp* must be the Japanese edition of *VAMP* magazine.

'It's so great to meet you two!' Reiko said, bouncing in her seat. 'And it is so nice of you to take care of me while I'm in Franklin Grove. This is a big adventure for me, you know?'

'It's no problem. Really.' Ivy didn't have to force a smile. Reiko may have been a little over-energetic, but she did seem like a nice person. 'I'm sure the next two weeks will be killer.'

'Absolutely.' Reiko's knee jiggled up and down so vigorously, Ivy had to scoot further to the side to keep from being bumped. 'So, who's playing tonight?'

'Um . . .?' Ivy gave Olivia a *Help-me!* look. 'None of the bands I know . . . Olivia?'

Ivy's twin shrugged.

'Not *music*.' Reiko laughed. 'No way! But Franklin Grove has a sports team, right?'

'Well . . .' Ivy's head was whirling.

'You must have *lots*,' Reiko said. 'There are so many different sports in America, right? Just like in Japan. So, who's playing tonight? And what time does the game start?'

Dread settled in Ivy's stomach. *No one warned me I'd have to watch sports for this!* 'I . . . have to check

13

the newspaper,' she said weakly. 'I think . . . are the sports reports at the back? Maybe?'

Olivia only shrugged again. Reiko looked stunned.

'Are you serious?' she said. 'I can't believe you two live in *America* and you don't follow sports!' She shook her head at both of them. 'If I lived here, I'd go to a different game every night!'

Please not for the next two weeks, Ivy begged silently. *I might start looking for a stake to walk into!*

As Reiko launched into an excited list of all the different types of games she most wanted to watch while she was in Franklin Grove, Ivy sagged lower and lower in her seat. *Does she actually expect me to watch a whole sports game? On purpose?*

Worse yet . . . based on how packed full of equipment that backpack was, Reiko might even expect Ivy to *play sports with her.*

Ivy shuddered. *I can't believe this is happening!*

14

Of all the possible vamps that she had imagined turning up, she would *never* have expected a sports fanatic! Now, here she was sitting right next to one . . . who suddenly gave her a nudge so powerful, she nearly slammed into the wall of their booth.

'Hey, do you mind if we go somewhere else for lunch?' Reiko tossed down the menu with a shudder. 'This whole menu is *really* unhealthy. Does the Meat and Greet have something against proper nutrients?'

'Ahem.' Next to the table, the waitress cleared her throat loudly.

Cringing, Ivy looked up. The waitress stood holding Olivia's diet soda . . . and she'd obviously heard every one of Reiko's words about the menu.

'Ready to order, *finally*?' the waitress snapped.

Ivy gave her best "apologetic" smile. 'Um . . . can we please have the check?'

The waitress let out a growl. 'I don't believe this!'

Ivy sighed. *Trust me, neither do I.*

🦇   🦇   🦇

Two hours later, Olivia led Ivy and Reiko through the echoing halls of the Franklin Grove Museum. She had to hold on to Ivy's elbow to keep her twin moving in the right direction. Ivy was walking backwards, her horrified gaze firmly fixed on the exchange student behind them . . .

Less than a minute after stepping into the museum, Reiko had pulled a tennis ball from her backpack. Now, she juggled it fluidly between her palms, elbows and shoulders as she walked. She was obviously skilled, but Olivia dreaded what would happen if the museum's intense vampire caretaker, Albert, caught sight of what was going on. And if Reiko's ball actually crashed into one of the museum's priceless displays?

Ouch. Olivia cringed at the idea.

16

Reiko was the only one who seemed completely unfazed by the priceless antiquities all around them. ' . . . and after we go to the basketball game,' she was saying, 'I want to see a *real* American football game! And then . . .'

'I can't take this any more,' Ivy mumbled. She pulled free of Olivia and turned to stride ahead.

Oh, dear. Olivia sighed. She couldn't imagine Ivy sitting through a single sports game, much less two weeks' worth of them!

Still, she didn't want Reiko to feel snubbed, so Olivia dropped behind to walk by the exchange student's side as she chattered on and on, juggling her tennis ball all the way. As they walked past an ancient ceramic vase sitting on a pedestal, the ball flew up over their heads. Reiko jumped up to catch it between her shoulder and jaw . . .

She missed.

'Oh!' Olivia gasped as the ball hurtled towards the vase.

'Noooo!' Albert suddenly appeared from the shadows of the hall, lunging towards them with his arms outstretched.

Ivy spun around. Horror spread across her face as she leaped forwards . . .

And, just in time, Reiko snatched the ball out of the air in a quick, backwards catch. 'There!' She winked at the others, grinning. 'You weren't worried, were you? I never miss a catch.'

Albert put one hand to his chest, as if to soothe his racing heart. He took deep breaths. Olivia thought he might be about to pass out from shock. As soon as he had calmed down, though, they were going to be in *big* trouble.

She traded a panicked look with Ivy. 'Let's hurry, OK?' *I don't want to be here when Albert starts yelling!* Putting one hand on Reiko's back, she steered the exchange student through the marble halls at a quick trot. Aiming a wary look back at the recovering caretaker, she tried to laugh. 'Sooo,

Reiko . . . I guess maybe you shouldn't have had that second cup of Vitali-Tea at lunch, huh?'

'Are you joking?' Reiko shook her head so vigorously, her long purple ponytail whipped against Olivia's cheek. 'That One Planet place you guys found is great! They even had gotu kola in the Vitali-Tea!'

Olivia glanced to Ivy for help, but her twin only shrugged.

'Gotu kola is one of my vices,' Reiko said happily. 'It's much better for you than caffeine, you know.'

'If you say so.' Smiling weakly, Olivia pushed open the door to the old South Wing. *Finally.* 'Ta-da! Check out Café Creative!'

'Cool!' Reiko didn't stop juggling, but she looked around with obvious interest.

Olivia felt a wave of pride as she followed the exchange student's gaze around the wide hall that her vampire stepmom had decked out so

19

impressively. 'Isn't it great? Lillian's done fantastic work with the space in here.'

Once, this whole wing of the museum had been abandoned and full of dust. Now, light beamed in through long windows, showing off the tables arranged in star-formations around an X-shaped platform.

Olivia pointed to it. 'See? That's going to be the catwalk for the fashion show this week.'

'Really?' Ivy groaned. 'It's raised, like, five feet off the ground. If I fall off that, I'll leave a dent in the floor!'

Laughter sounded behind them, and a familiar female voice spoke: 'Now, I *know* you're more graceful than that, Ivy Vega!'

Olivia, Ivy and Reiko all spun around . . . and for the first time since they'd stepped into the museum, Reiko actually dropped her tennis ball. It bounced away across the floor and rolled underneath the catwalk, but she didn't even seem to notice. Her mouth had fallen open and her eyes were wide as she stared at the two new arrivals standing in the doorway: a young man with spiky black hair and high cheekbones, and a young woman with long, silky black hair tied in an impossibly long braid.

'Is this . . .' Reiko stopped and swallowed visibly. 'I mean, are you *really* . . . can you be . . . Prince Alex and Princess Tessa of Transylvania?'

Olivia hid a grin. Who knew the sports-mad vampire could be so star-struck?

'Of course they are,' she said warmly, and ran forwards to hug them. 'What are you guys *doing* here?'

'We're on, um . . . *official* business,' said Alex, giving Ivy a hug. 'But we couldn't come all this way and not swing by to visit our favourite twins!'

'Just look at you!' Olivia exclaimed, moving to hug Tessa. 'You're such a princess now!'

Tessa laughed as she gave Olivia a careful hug,

holding a thin wooden box to one side. 'It took a lot of training,' she whispered. 'But the Queen is finally pleased with me.'

'Of course she is.' Smiling, Olivia stepped back and looked her friend over. With the grace and poise in every line of Tessa's posture, no one would ever recognise the timid serving girl the twins had first met. 'Married life really suits you!'

Tessa smiled, her cheeks flushing. 'I think it does!'

'Watch out!' The strained voice belonged to Camilla Edmunson, Olivia's best friend. 'Wardrobe coming through!'

As the others all scattered to make way, Camilla and Lillian staggered into the room, pushing a tall, intricately carved oak wardrobe on a wheeled platform. Normally, Lillian's vamp-strength would have been enough for her to carry it by herself with ease, but she had to keep up the act of 'being human' in front of bunnies like Camilla.

She also looked *genuinely* exhausted.

'What do we still have to do?' Lillian rasped, as she and Camilla heaved the wardrobe across the room. 'Do the caterers have their menu?'

'Done,' Camilla panted as they shoved the platform the last few steps forward.

'The news releases are all sent out?'

'Done.'

'And the short film?'

'Um . . .' Camilla shook her head, looking shifty, as she let go of the platform's handle. 'Not quite done yet.'

Lillian winced. 'Camilla, this film is supposed to be playing on loop all through Wednesday evening,' she said. 'That's just *four days* from now. Is everything OK?'

'It's just not quite perfect yet!' Camilla ran one hand through her short, springy blonde curls, her face scrunching into what Olivia called her 'artistic scowl'. 'I'm still editing, but I swear I *will* lock the picture very soon. It just needs a few more touches!'

'Well, in that case . . .' Lillian raised her eyebrows. 'Why don't you go home and finish up now?'

'Oh, no, I can stay and help here some more first,' Camilla said. 'I'll just –'

'Camilla,' Lillian said, smiling although there was worry in her eyes. 'I need that film to be turned in by the end of tonight . . . perfect or not!'

Camilla winced. 'It *will* be perfect. I swear it. No matter what it takes!'

With a hasty wave at the others, she grabbed her purple velvet beret from inside the wardrobe and darted out of the room.

Lillian sighed and looked around the space, her shoulders hunching.

24

'Last-minute concerns?' Tessa asked sympathetically.

'Oh . . .' Lillian gave an unconvincing smile as she walked over to join Olivia and the vampires. She was dressed just as elegantly as usual, in a black pantsuit and discreet pearls, but she looked as if she needed to sleep in her coffin for at least a month. 'I'm just really nervous about the opening.'

'It's going to be great,' Olivia said.

'It really will,' Ivy added. 'Seriously. Even *I* think this space looks . . .' She winced, then forced the word out with an obvious effort: '. . . Fabulous!'

'Well, in *that* case . . .' Lillian's lips twitched. She looped one arm around Ivy's shoulder and gave it a squeeze.

'Luckily,' Tessa announced firmly, 'there is no need to be nervous, because . . . look what I brought!' She held out the wooden box she'd been carrying.

Lillian blinked at it. 'What – oh!' Her face lit up. 'I remember! Charles said that you were going to loan us the pashmina you wore at your wedding reception. That is wonderful!'

'Ooh! I want to see it!' Olivia couldn't help almost barging Ivy aside to get a better look as their stepmom opened the narrow box. A fabulous, blood-red pashmina lay folded inside, embroidered with bat symbols in a mix of black and gold. The colours were so rich and vibrant, the pashmina seemed to glow against the wood.

Olivia gasped. 'Tessa, that's gorgeous!'

'That is one of the coolest things I've ever seen,' Reiko agreed. She started to reach out as if to touch it – then yanked her hand back as if she'd been burned.

Alex smiled proudly, wrapping one arm around his wife's waist. 'It was a gift from the Indian vampire community's Senior Ambassador,' he explained. 'It is said to bring good fortune to

26

whoever holds it close. Franklin Grove Museum will have it on display until the spring. While it is here, nothing bad can happen. So, you see? There's nothing to worry about.'

'Oh, thank darkness.' Lillian visibly relaxed for the first time that day. 'I can't tell you how much this helps.'

As Olivia looked at her stepmom's relieved expression, she had to stifle a giggle. *Vampires really are* so *superstitious!*

Chapter Two

Olivia was in such a rush to get to her locker at the end of school on Wednesday, she had to make a quick, dancing side-step to avoid the stooped, elderly janitor who stood in her way. With only a few hours to go before the grand opening of Café Creative, she didn't have much time – she'd have to rush home if she wanted to scoff down a quick sandwich before heading over to the museum.

As she bundled her books into her locker, a familiar *clump-clump-clump* caught her attention.

It was the unmistakable noise of Amelia

Thompson's heavy black boots marching down the hall.

Olivia glanced around curiously. The gothabulous senior was making a bee-line for Penny Taylor. Penny was a bunny freshman who had once pretended to be the gothiest of goths – but actually preferred the lighter, sparklier side of life. Today, Penny looked as bright as spring in a blue cardigan and pale pink dress . . . and Amelia was scowling as she marched towards her.

Uh-oh. Forgetting her own hurry for a moment, Olivia turned around to get a better look. *Is Amelia mad at Penny about something?*

Both Penny and Amelia were designers for the fashion show at the Café's grand opening, and Olivia just knew Lillian would be devastated if anything fell apart at the last minute.

Amelia came to a halt in front of the younger girl. 'Is *it* ready?' she demanded.

'Oh, yes.' Penny gave a satisfied smile. 'I finished up the very last piece over lunch break. It is *definitely* ready . . . and it's *definitely* going to be great!'

'Ohh!' Amelia *wasn't* mad at Penny at all. Olivia couldn't help herself. Leaving her locker door hanging open, she rushed forwards, side-stepping around the janitor again to race towards the other girls.

'Please!' she begged, as she arrived at Penny's locker. 'I've been dying to know about this show-stopping secret project. What *did* you guys collaborate on? I know it must have been a dress, or . . . well . . . *some* item of clothing, right?' She looked from one of them to the other, lowering her voice as a group of chattering students passed behind her. 'Come on, can't you just give me a hint?'

Penny laughed. 'It's a *secret*, Olivia!'

'Yes, but I'm one of your models,' Olivia said.

'So you don't have to keep it a secret from *me*!'

Penny and Amelia traded a look. Despite their differences in style, when they turned back to face Olivia, they wore exactly the same teasing grin.

'You'll just have to wait and see, like everybody else,' Amelia said sternly.

'But . . .' Olivia began.

Penny giggled as she closed her locker. 'The one thing we *can* tell you is: it's really kind of . . .'

'"Altegular"!' Amelia finished.

They both burst into laughter as they linked arms and walked away down the hall, leaving Olivia staring after them.

'Altegular'? What does that mean?

'Excuse me.' It was the janitor again, his voice gruff and his face hidden under a ragged old baseball cap as he stepped up to mop the floor around Olivia's feet.

'Oh, sorry.' Sighing, Olivia started to head back to her own locker.

Then she stopped. *Wait a minute.* The janitor wasn't stooped any more. In fact, she was certain she *recognised* his posture from somewhere . . .

Narrowing her eyes, she turned to stare at him. Lowering his mop, he turned right back to her and raised the brim of his cap.

Olivia's breath stopped in her throat. *That's no janitor!*

Even with make-up carefully applied to 'age up' his face, she would have known those blue eyes anywhere.

It was her far-too-famous boyfriend, Jackson Caulfield!

'Oh, *really*.' Olivia tried to scowl, but she couldn't help laughing. 'Has your career really slipped this far, Jackson? Is Amy getting you cleaning jobs now between shoots?'

'Ahem.' Still speaking in his gruff, old man's voice, Jackson gave a wink. 'I don't think you should be openly flirting with a school janitor, do you?'

'Whatever.' Rolling her eyes, Olivia walked back to her locker and pushed the door wide open, so that no one else could see her expression. 'So,' she said, through the locker door, 'what *are* you doing here, really?'

'What do you think?' Groups of students walked past behind them, but Jackson's voice was too low for any of them to overhear. 'I got into town early, and I wanted to see you. But for obvious reasons, it didn't seem like a good idea to be noticed coming into the school.'

'Hmm.' Olivia raised her eyebrows. 'Do you know, I think there's a part of you that actually *enjoys* the trouble you can cause!'

'I just like the practice,' Jackson said cheerfully. 'It's good to try out different roles.' He shifted to mop the floor on her other side. 'So, what time does the event start tonight?'

'Seven-thirty,' Olivia said. It was a good reminder: she started packing her bag as she spoke. 'Just remember, you can expect some chaos as we try to get into the museum.'

'That's fine.' Jackson shrugged. 'It can't be any tougher than that crowd at the premiere for *The Groves* . . . remember?'

'How could I forget?' She remembered feeling like she might pass out from the crowds pressing in on them that evening. Their excitement had been overwhelming.

'Just wait,' Jackson said. 'I bet the one we have for "ES" is going to be an even bigger deal.'

'Oh.' Olivia gulped. *I hadn't even thought of that.*

Jackson was talking about *Eternal Sunset*, the film they were currently shooting. At its premiere, Olivia would be walking the red carpet as the *lead* actress of a major movie for the very first time – and it would be the last time for at least five years, since she'd made the choice to put her acting career on hold until she had finished high school.

Would her big moment at the premiere feel exciting? Or just bittersweet?

Uh-oh. She suddenly realised that Jackson had been talking through her moment of distraction. 'Huh?'

'Olivia Abbott, are you *bored* of me already?' He raised his cap to give her a look of mock-offence.

She lightly swatted his arm. 'You know that's not it!'

Then she blushed, as she looked up and caught at least three other students staring at her from around the corridor. *I guess they weren't expecting to see me hit an elderly janitor. Oops!*

'I was just saying, it won't be long before we've wrapped on "ES",' said Jackson. 'Final scenes shoot in November.'

'Right.' Olivia sighed. Life would become so much easier once she didn't have to balance schoolwork and filming any more . . . but she couldn't be *completely* happy about that, because it would mean she'd get much less time with Jackson.

'Anyway . . . I'll see you tonight.' He glanced left and right under the brim of his cap and nodded decisively. 'I'd better get back to work. I see a corner over there that's *filthy*.'

'What are you *doing*?' Olivia stared at him as he started forward. 'You're not actually *paid* to clean the school, remember?'

Jackson shrugged. 'I can never leave a job unfinished. Anyway, you probably ought to rescue Ivy.'

'Rescue —? What are you talking about?'

'Oh, I couldn't possibly ruin the surprise.' Jackson gave her a wry, amused grin. 'You have to take a walk across the quad and see this one for yourself. Besides, you wouldn't believe me if I did tell you!'

It was such a familiar grin – and she'd missed him so much – that Olivia couldn't help herself. She started forwards, her arms rising instinctively . . .

Then she pulled herself back, just in time. *No way.* It was weird enough for her to be seen hitting the janitor. If anyone saw her *hug* him, too, then they would *really* have questions!

So she only whispered, 'Later,' smiled, and turned away.

Time to rescue Ivy – whatever that means!

She hurried down the hall towards the quad, ignoring the students shooting her curious glances. As she stepped outside into the cloudy autumn afternoon, though, she was startled to see the *actual* janitor, Jonny, leaning against an outer wall and taking deep breaths.

'Um . . .' Hesitantly, she started towards him. She'd never spoken to him before, but she couldn't just ignore his distress. 'Excuse me, but

37

are you OK? You don't look very well.'

Hastily straightening, Jonny smoothed down his grey hair with shaking fingers. 'I feel like I'm going crazy,' he mumbled. 'I've been walking the halls of this school for the last twenty minutes, getting ready to begin my end-of-the-day work, but . . .' He shook his head in disbelief. 'They're already *spotless*! Either I've come down with serious amnesia, or the students have actually started cleaning up after themselves . . . and I don't know what would be scarier!'

Stifling a laugh, Olivia ducked her head so that he couldn't read her expression. 'Um . . . the teachers did ask us all to respect the school a bit more,' she mumbled, and moved away quickly, before he could say anything else.

As she walked across the quad, she kept her eyes open for Ivy, looking left and right, past groups of goths and bunnies and . . .

No. I can't believe it! Gasping, Olivia came to a

sudden halt as she finally spotted her twin sister.

I know Ivy's been struggling to keep Reiko entertained . . . but I would never have expected this!

🦇   🦇   🦇

Ivy spotted Olivia out of the corner of her eye, but she couldn't wave, because her hands were full. She couldn't even nod at her sister, because she had to keep her eyes on the ball, of all ridiculous things.

She was trapped playing *doubles tennis*!

'Ivy and Reiko lead by four games to love,' called the sophomore bunny who'd volunteered as their umpire. She sounded as excited as if she was watching a professional tennis match.

I can't believe this is happening to me, Ivy thought miserably.

Reiko had insisted they play against Skylar Drew and Hayley Winston, two blonde bunny seniors who were tennis-obsessed. Both girls were super-athletic, and had promised to 'go easy' on

39

the two freshmen girls but the truth was, they had very little hope of beating two vampires . . . even if one of those vampires didn't even *like* tennis.

Why couldn't I just say no? Ivy asked herself. But she already knew the answer.

She couldn't be mean to the exchange student. Unfortunately, tactful dodges didn't seem to work with Reiko; and Reiko – whose hair was a vivid blue today – apparently could *not* walk past the tennis court without challenging the girls already there to a ferocious game of doubles.

Now, Reiko fired a fast forehand that had Skylar scrambling to return. Ivy swung a half-hearted backhand . . . but a *vampire's* half-hearted backhand still sent the ball flying across the court so fast it was almost invisible.

Hayley lunged forwards just in time to return the ball with a clever drop shot. It fell just over the net, and Skylar hooted with triumph before it could even land.

'Yes!'

No normal player could possibly get to that ball in time . . . but Reiko was no normal player. She raced forwards in a green-yellow-and-blue blur to dive, racquet first and flick the ball back up and over the heads of their opponents. Hayley and Skylar collided into each other as they both leaped for it, collapsing in a tangle of tanned arms and legs.

'Fifteen-love,' the umpire announced, staring at Reiko in amazement.

Ouch. Ivy felt a wave of sympathy as she watched the bunnies pick themselves up, groaning. 'Let's take a minute, OK?' she called out. 'I'm, um, out of breath.'

Hayley and Skylar only waved their assent, panting too hard to talk.

Ivy pulled Reiko aside and lowered her voice to a whisper. 'Hey, cut it out with the super-vamp moves. We're supposed to be making this game competitive, remember?'

'No way.' Reiko grinned. 'I'm here to *win*.'

'We already *are* winning,' Ivy hissed. 'Plus, if you make any more plays like that last one, we're going to get some serious questions. A normal human being can't *do* things like that!'

Reiko shrugged. 'I'll take my game down to ninety-five per cent, but that's the best I can do.'

Ivy groaned as they took their places once more.

The bunny girls both looked grimly determined to re-balance the score. Skylar fired in a serve that, by human standards, would have been considered "fierce".

Ivy faked a sneeze, dropping her racquet, and the ball whistled past her head.

'Fifteen-all,' the umpire declared.

'No *way*!' Reiko shouted. 'Ivy, how could you miss that?'

Even the bunnies were frowning. 'You

42

definitely would have gotten that, if you hadn't had to sneeze,' Skylar said. 'Do you want to replay the point?'

'No.' Ivy shook her head emphatically. 'It's yours, fair and square.'

'If you say so . . .' Skylar looked worried.

Reiko just looked outraged. She shot Ivy a narrow-eyed look, then took her place, ready to receive the next serve.

This time, Skylar hit the ball just as fiercely as before – but Reiko returned it with a double-backhand that burned through the air.

'Aaahh!' Hayley fell to the ground with a scream of pain. The ball had hit her on the knee.

'Time out,' the umpire said. 'I guess.'

Ivy threw aside her racquet to leap over the net and crouch beside Hayley. 'Are you OK?'

'I . . . I . . . *ow*!' Hayley let out a moan of agony as Skylar gently massaged her knee. She closed her eyes, taking deep, ragged breaths as a whispering crowd gathered on the court. 'I don't think I can get up by myself,' she mumbled.

'She needs a doctor!' Skylar said.

'I know first aid!' called the umpire, running over.

Good. Ivy's shoulders relaxed. That meant she was free to deal with the *other* problem.

Ivy turned and shot Reiko a surreptitious death-squint.

'*What were you thinking?*' she mouthed.

Reiko shrugged sheepishly, but Ivy didn't spot any *real* regret on her face. Apparently, Reiko figured that losing the ability to walk was just an occupational hazard for anyone who was foolish enough to play tennis with her.

Gritting her teeth, Ivy started towards the other vampire . . .

But a cry of anguish shattered the air behind her, making her spin around.

The sound came not from Hayley, but from

Amelia Thompson, who had shoved her way through the crowd to Olivia's side. 'She can't *walk*?' Amelia demanded. 'Is that *true*?'

'Sorry.' Hayley just barely managed to raise herself up on her elbows, with Skylar's help. 'I know you were expecting me at the fashion show tonight, Amelia, but –'

'I wasn't just *expecting* you,' Amelia said. 'I *need* you there! You're modelling our "Altegular" outfit tonight!'

Hayley looked like she might be blinking back tears. 'I don't think I'll even be able to sit in the audience for the fashion show, much less strut down that catwalk.'

'Ahh . . . ahhh . . .!' Amelia looked as if she might faint. She grabbed out at Olivia for support.

If it weren't for Hayley's pain, and her own anger at Reiko's carelessness, Ivy might have almost found it funny. She had *never* seen Amelia get so emotional about *anything*.

Reiko jogged over, swinging her tennis racquet by her side. 'It's my fault Hayley can't do it,' she said. 'So, can I help? I could be her stand-in, if you need one.'

'A stand-in?' Amelia straightened, looking Reiko up and down. The despair in her eyes seemed to fade. 'Yes . . . You *might* work. You're about the right size, and I assume you can walk without falling over?'

Reiko raised her eyebrows, obviously taking it as a challenge. Tossing her racquet up into the air, she strutted forwards across the tennis court, catching it seven steps later – while twirling gracefully. 'How's that?'

'Well . . .' Amelia's eyes narrowed. 'It's a bit more . . . *forceful* than I'd like, but I guess I can't be choosy this close to showtime.'

'Excellent.' Reiko grinned.

'Wait!' Amelia snapped. 'Your hair might not work.'

'Oh, don't worry about that.' Reiko shrugged. 'I can change it to any colour you want.'

'Hmm.' Amelia considered her. 'Something dark would be best. Maybe black or . . . no, wait – blood red!'

'You want red,' Reiko said cheerfully, 'you'll have red!'

'Ohhh . . .' Looking uncharacteristically misty-eyed, Amelia wrapped the exchange student in a hug. 'Such school *spirit* from someone who's only going to be here for two weeks. We're so lucky to have you!'

I'm not sure Hayley would agree, Ivy thought.

Amelia's phone rang, and she scooped it out of her black leather satchel. As she strode away in her heavy boots, Ivy's vampire-strong hearing picked up Penny's voice on the other side of the call, sounding tinny through the cell phone's speakers.

'I heard about Hayley. Is she –?'

47

'It's all sorted out,' Amelia said. 'Don't worry.'

Reiko turned to Ivy with a big grin. 'I get to model . . . I am having *so* much fun at this school!'

'Seriously?' Ivy stared at her.

Reiko was super-sporty, scarily competitive, *and* excited by the idea of a fashion show? Ivy sighed. *We're not just from different countries . . . I think we may actually come from different planets!*

Chapter Three

That evening, as Jackson's black limousine drove down the street towards Franklin Grove Museum, Olivia looked out through one dark, smoky window and shook her head in disbelief.

Until now, she had always thought of museums as *quiet* places – but tonight, Franklin Grove Museum was a hub of sheer *noise*. Cameras flashed to capture images of the people filing into the building. On either side of the small aisle on the pavement, matching crowds of teenaged girls were pressed against the safety barriers that lined the kerb for about fifty yards in both directions.

They seemed to be buzzing with anticipation. Inside the limo, Olivia had to take a deep breath to calm down and prepare herself for the event ahead.

As they pulled up outside the museum, the crowd's chant drifted into the vehicle. 'Jack-son! Jack-son! Jack-son!'

Crowds of teens lunged towards the car, arms outstretched, and a line of hard-faced security men stepped forwards to make sure no one could climb over the barriers.

Cameras flashed as journalists and photographers spotted the limo and raced in to focus on it.

Jackson squeezed Olivia's fingers, grinning. 'Excited?'

'I am,' Olivia said. *But I don't know about the others!*

Sitting on the long seat across from them, Ivy and her boyfriend, Brendan, looked frozen with horror as they took in the pandemonium outside their little local museum. Olivia could barely believe she had lived in Franklin Grove for over a year before finding out it existed!

After tonight, everyone *will know it's here*, Olivia thought proudly. *Thanks to Lillian and Jackson!*

Ivy sounded like she was choking as she spoke. 'Now I know why you made us dress up, even though we'll just have to change into different fancy clothes once we're inside.'

'Yeah, well, it's all right for you,' Brendan said nervously. 'You look great, but I'm just wearing my regular clothes.'

On Ivy's other side, Reiko didn't say a word. Her eyes had been wide and glazed-looking ever since the beginning of the ride, when she'd first seen exactly who was sitting across from her. Even now, she seemed to be far too busy staring at Jackson to come up with a coherent thought. As far as Olivia could tell, Reiko hadn't even noticed the chaos outside.

She's even more freaked out by Jackson than she was by vampire royalty!

Olivia smiled as she took in Reiko's petrified expression. Meeting Alex and Tessa and then a movie star was probably a lot more than Reiko had been expecting on a simple exchange programme to a quiet little American town!

'So, are you guys ready?' Jackson asked.

'No!' Ivy said. 'But . . . that doesn't really matter, does it?' She took a breath, obviously bracing herself. 'Let's do this.' She leaned forwards to reach for the door handle.

Olivia grabbed her arm to stop her. 'That's not a good idea.'

'Oh, I know!' Ivy said, letting out a panicky half-laugh. 'It's a *crazy* idea for me to be modelling – but what choice do I have?'

Olivia gently nudged Ivy back into her seat. 'That's not what I meant. If anyone but Jackson is first out of this limo, they will risk *serious* hearing

52

loss. It's much better for us to walk in Jackson's slipstream and save our ears.'

Brendan frowned. 'But what about Jackson?'

'Don't worry about me.' Grinning, Jackson reached into the pockets of his black trousers and took out a pair of earplugs. He stuck them in, then clapped his hands together. 'All right, let's go!'

Brendan reached out to open the limo door for Jackson – and the noise from the crowd rushed in like a surge of floodwater.

Beaming his famous, megawatt grin, Jackson slid out of the limo, raising his hands high to greet the crowd outside.

One . . . two . . . three . . . Olivia counted down, then stepped out after him, surreptitiously smoothing down her floaty pink chiffon gown and slipping into his wake with the three vamps close behind her.

Cameras flashed in her eyes. Screams sounded

just ahead. It was overwhelming, it was scary . . . and Olivia could not stop smiling. Lillian's pet project had become a *huge* deal!

As Ivy, Brendan and Reiko ducked their heads to race as fast as possible into the museum, journalists swarmed Olivia and Jackson.

'Just a quick interview!'

'Please, one moment of your time!'

'Of course,' Jackson said easily. He nodded to Albert, who stood holding the museum's front door open, and the vampire caretaker stepped back, making space. Jackson came to a smooth stop at the top of the museum's front steps, slipping his arm around Olivia's waist. 'We're happy to stop and talk, aren't we?'

'Of course,' Olivia said. But she had to swallow a gulp as countless mics suddenly swarmed around their heads like giant, multi-coloured flies.

Questions flew at them from all sides, forcing her to constantly swing her head back and forth,

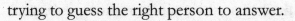

trying to guess the right person to answer.

'Tell us all about your relationship!'

'Your fans want to know – are you two lovebirds back together for good this time?'

'What did you eat for dinner tonight?'

'Do you have any relationship advice?'

'Tell us: are you excited about *Eternal Sunset*?'

Olivia wished she could be as good at this sort of thing as Jackson. He always had great answers – even to the silly questions! Still, she knew the basic rule of interviews: *keep to the main topic!*

'Of course we're excited about *Eternal Sunset*,' she said, 'but that won't come out for another year, and tonight is all about the opening of Café Creative! It's a fantastic new achievement for Lillian Vega.' Putting on her best 'Hollywood' smile, Olivia turned to beam directly into every hovering camera in turn. 'She's had a successful career in Hollywood, and is now devoting herself to nurturing young, local talent. Jackson and I both think that she's super inspiring. Everyone from Franklin Grove – and anyone else in driving distance – should totally come by and check out Café Creative!'

'But, Jackson! *Jackson!*' One reporter in a bright yellow jacket pushed his way forwards, elbowing everyone else aside roughly. He shoved his mic in Jackson's face. '*Are* you going to take the role in the first *Wanderer* movie?'

'Well, maybe,' Jackson began, stepping back, 'but tonight –'

'And is it true that Jessica Phelps is begging for your help in repairing her tattered career?' the reporter demanded, stepping even closer.

Jackson winced and raised one hand to hold the man off. 'No, that isn't true. Now, if you guys will all excuse us . . .' Jackson nodded to Albert, who hovered by the door, and the vampire caretaker swung it open just wide enough for the two of them.

56

A chorus of disappointment sounded from the crowd, but Jackson only smiled. 'Tonight's a big night for one of my favourite towns, and it's a great honour to be asked to attend the opening. I hope you guys all have fun!' Taking Olivia's hand, he led her into the museum, leaving the reporters shouting final, unanswered questions behind them.

'Whew!' Olivia let out a sigh of relief as Albert closed the door behind them. 'I thought I might pass out!'

'You'll get used to it,' Jackson said. He squeezed her hand as they walked together through the echoing museum hallways, leaving Albert behind and heading towards the sound of laughter and conversation far ahead.

Olivia tipped her head against his shoulder, savouring this moment. It was so rare for them to be alone together, she felt like she could walk by his side forever, just enjoying the feel of his strong fingers laced through hers and his shoulder warm against her cheek.

All too soon, though, they were walking through the doorway of Café Creative, which was bustling with preparations for the opening – it was just an hour away now. Lillian had lined all four walls with fabulous paintings by young, local artists. A few special guests were milling around the room, drinking sparkling grape juice and admiring the artwork.

Olivia stood up on tiptoes to give Jackson a quick, sweet kiss. 'I've got to head "backstage" to get ready for the fashion show. Wish me luck?'

'Of course. But . . .' For once, Jackson looked uncertain. 'Do I say "break a leg" in this situation? I'm not sure that would be such a good idea for someone who's about to do a lot of *very important walking*!'

Olivia laughed as she stepped away from him. 'Just a simple "good luck" should be fine.'

'Well, you don't need luck,' Jackson told her, catching her hand for one last moment. 'Because you are an *excellent* walker.'

'Hmm.' Olivia rolled her eyes at him as she pulled free . . . but she couldn't help beaming as she walked away from him.

I have the best boyfriend!

She headed towards the smaller café area, already feeling curiosity start to bubble up inside her. It was almost time for her to finally see Amelia and Penny's "Altegular" design – whatever that meant – and she couldn't wait!

Then she saw the group just behind the café counter, and she came to a dead halt. *Uh-oh*. It was her bio-dad, Charles, standing with Amelia and Penny – and from the desperate expressions on the girls' faces, it looked as if they were actually *pleading* with him about something!

Olivia's kitten heels clicked purposefully against the tiled floor as she started forwards . . .

59

and as she arrived, she realised she'd been just in time. *Uh-oh*. Her bio-dad might be as neat as ever in a tailored black suit, but he was tapping his hand so nervously against the café counter, he might leave a dent in it at any moment with his vampire-strength!

'Dad!' She grabbed his hand, subtly pulling it away from danger.

'Olivia.' He gave her a brief, grateful look before he turned back to the others. 'I'm really not sure about this . . .' he began.

'I *promise*,' Amelia said. 'No damage will come to the pashmina!'

'The *what*?' Olivia's eyes widened. 'Wait a minute. Are you guys thinking of incorporating Alex and Tessa's wedding pashmina into the show?'

'It will be fine,' Penny said quickly. 'Honestly. I know it sounds a little crazy, but –'

'It sounds *fabulous*!' Olivia gave a bounce of

excitement, her chiffon dress fluttering around her. 'Dad, you have to let them! They've worked so hard on their outfits, and I just know they'll be amazing – the kind of "amazing" that will have everyone talking about Café Creative. Lillian's project will have the best possible start . . .'

'Well . . .' Charles pursed his lips, seemingly torn between his eagerness to help his new wife, and his duty to a precious vampire artefact. 'We must take the *greatest* care of the pashmina.'

'And that's exactly what we'd be doing by using it tonight!' Olivia gave his hand an excited squeeze. 'Don't you remember what you said when you decided to make use of the museum for Café Creative? That we would be *showcasing the art of tomorrow as well as yesterday.* Well, how amazing would it be to help the fashion of tomorrow pay tribute to the fashion of yesterday *tonight*?'

. . . And I really hope that last line made some *sense,* she added ruefully to herself. Nerves fluttered in

her chest as she searched her bio-dad's face. In the corner of her eye, she could see Amelia and Penny looking frozen with anticipation.

Finally, Charles's lips curved into a real smile. 'Very well.' He nodded graciously to Amelia and Penny. 'The pashmina is yours for tonight . . . But you *must* be careful. Should any damage come to it, *you* will be the ones answering to Albert!'

Penny cringed, and even Amelia winced at the threat of the stern caretaker. But that didn't stop her from giving a firm nod. 'Don't worry,' she said. 'This is going to be great!'

Linking arms, the two girls hurried off to collect the pashmina from the display room, Amelia's big black boots stomping in time with Penny's delicate blue satin high heels.

Charles gave Olivia a fond smile.

Grinning back, she tugged him down so she could kiss his cheek. 'Thanks, Dad. I'll see you later – I have a fashion show to prepare for!'

'And a twin sister to reassure, I expect,' Charles added. 'I'd hurry, if I were you.'

'Good point!' Olivia stepped away hastily, walking as quickly as her heels would let her all the rest of the way through the café.

Ivy hadn't been happy about the fashion show from the beginning. Now that it was actually time for her to put on a designer outfit and strut onstage, she would definitely need some sisterly support!

Olivia pushed open the door to the staff break room that was functioning as "backstage" for the night . . . and came to a dead halt.

The room was pitch black. *Am I in the right place?*

A sudden faint glow lit up in the back of the room for a moment, followed by another glow in a different corner. Neither of them was bright enough for her to see who or what had made the light.

'Is anyone here?' Olivia called softly.

'Unfortunately.' Ivy's sigh echoed through the room. 'Close the door! We're in the middle of getting changed.'

'Ohh-kaayyy . . .' Hesitantly, Olivia stepped inside, closing the door behind her. Blindly, she reached out with both arms to check for obstacles in her way, apologising as she bumped into other models. 'Is there a reason nobody's turned on the lights?'

'They're not working,' Reiko called. Her voice sounded muffled, as if she was in the middle of pulling something over her head. 'Ivy thinks a fuse must have blown. All the other rooms seem to be OK. Someone's gone to look for Albert, but . . .'

'That could take forever.' Olivia sighed. 'He's busy guarding the front door right now. He won't be able to fix anything until the show's already in progress.'

'That's why we've all got started anyway. We're

over here,' Ivy called. 'Just follow my voice.'

It took a few moments of stumbling through darkness, bumping into models and tables along the way, but Olivia finally made her way to her twin sister, as two more faint glows swept through the darkness nearby. This time, she was close enough to see that they came from tiny cell-phone screens: the only light the girls had to help them find their clothes.

Ivy grumbled as she yanked her own dress over her head. 'If I step out into the light of the café and see I've put this thing on back-to-front, I swear I'll stake myself!'

Olivia giggled. 'Not before Amelia stakes you for ruining the effect of her dress!'

Reiko's infectious laugh sounded nearby. 'I love this! Everything in America is so . . . *dramatic.*'

There's one way to think of it. Smiling, Olivia pulled her own cell phone out of her small evening bag and aimed it at the rack where all the remaining dresses hung. It didn't help much, especially since the faint light only stayed on for a few seconds at a time, but luckily, she still remembered where her and Ivy's dresses had been hung up last night after the dress rehearsal.

It was hard to keep her smile, though, as she fought to change out of her chiffon gown and into the new one without tearing or wrinkling either dress – *or* dropping anything on to the floor to be trodden on by one of the other models!

Unfortunately, she had to set down her cell phone and evening bag to pull her new dress over her head. As she finally managed to work one arm through a sleeve, she reached out blindly to find the cell phone again – and toppled as she lost her balance in the darkness.

'Got you!' Ivy's strong hand snapped out to catch her.

Thank goodness for vampire reflexes! Olivia clutched at her sister's arm for balance . . . then frowned.

'Your sleeve is a little frilly tonight, isn't it?'

Ivy grunted. 'Amelia probably added the frills after last night's dress rehearsal, to lighten up her goth look. You know they've been *obsessively* fiddling with their designs over the last few days.'

'You're probably right.' Olivia nodded as she straightened, letting go of Ivy. 'She wouldn't want to contrast *too* dramatically with Penny's style, would she?'

The far door opened, letting in light and noise from outside. Both designers stood silhouetted in the doorway. 'Reiko?' Penny called. 'Are you in here?'

'We've got the pashmina!' Amelia announced. She cradled it in her arms as carefully as if she were handling a precious relic.

As the two designers closed the door and fumbled their way through the darkness towards Reiko, a sudden riot of noise sounded from outside.

'Sounds like all the rest of the guests are

finally being allowed into the café!' Olivia said. Excitement bubbled up inside her like sparkling water. This might be modelling, not acting, but still, this was her first live performance since Camilla's play, *Romezog and Julietron*. It felt even better than the nervous energy she got before every first take on a movie set!

In the distance, she heard the soundtrack of Camilla's short film playing for the assembled guests. *Soon, I'll get to watch the whole thing,* Olivia told herself. *But right now . . .*

Ivy sounded like she might be sick. 'I guess it's showtime.'

'Is everybody ready?' Amelia's voice barked through the darkness, sounding higher and shriller than usual. 'Make sure you're all lined up in the right order!'

'Ow!' Olivia gave a pained squeak as she bumped directly into a table's edge. 'That might be easier said than done!'

Stumbling through the darkness, the girls whispered their names to each other in order to find their places in the straggling line. They put their hands on each other's shoulders to keep the line linked through the pitch-black room.

'Reiko, make sure you're at the very back,' Penny called anxiously. 'Remember, our "Altegular" collaboration has to be saved for the grand finale!'

Olivia groaned. 'I can't believe I've been in this room with your big secret for the past fifteen minutes, and I still haven't even *seen* it!'

'Very, very soon!' Reiko carolled happily from the back of the line.

Just behind Olivia, her twin let out a very un-Ivy whimper.

'Ladies and gentlemen . . .' Lillian's voice sounded through the door, amplified through a microphone. 'Tonight we begin . . . with a fashion show!'

69

This is it! Olivia couldn't help giving a wiggle of excitement.

The runway music kicked in, blasting from speakers set around the stage, and Amelia pulled the "backstage" door open partway, just wide enough to let the models through without letting the crowd outside get any glimpses of what would be coming next.

As the music thumped through the building, shaking the walls of the dressing room, each model stepped in turn through the open doorway, heads high and postures perfect. As they passed, just enough light shone through the doorway to illuminate their dresses for the first time . . .

And Olivia sucked in a breath as she finally saw each dress in its final version. *Wow. These designs are amazing!* If Amelia and Penny were any sign of the calibre of young talents who would be flocking to Lillian's establishment after tonight, there was no doubt about it: Café Creative was going to be a hit!

Olivia heard a shaky sigh behind her. As the line continued to shuffle forwards, she turned and found Ivy's hand in the darkness. '*Don't* be nervous,' she said firmly.

'Me, nervous?' said Ivy, with a laugh that was a little too loud. 'I'm just getting myself into "graceful" mode, that's all.'

As the model in front of her stepped through the open door, Olivia gave Ivy's hands a gentle squeeze. Squinting through the darkness, she tried to take a good look at her sister's dress, but all she could see was a dull, pale shine in the shadows. Still . . . 'You have nothing to be afraid of. Remember? *No one* can pull off a fabulous goth look the way you can!'

'Go!' Amelia hissed, from the doorway, while Penny made shooing motions with her hand.

Putting on a wide, confident smile, Olivia

stepped through the doorway – and tried not to squint as bright light fell across her, after standing so long in the darkness.

Gasps sounded all around her as she strutted, half-blinded, toward the runway. Beneath the thumping music, she could hear murmurs of approval rising around her. *Whatever I'm wearing, they really think it looks fantastic!*

Olivia couldn't help it. She had to see what final modifications Penny had made to her design! As she stepped on to the runway, she quickly looked down at herself.

Then she jerked her gaze upright again just in time to stop herself from tripping. Her mind whirling, she fixed her smile even more brightly on her face and sauntered forwards, just as she'd practised in dress rehearsal.

The audience was right – she did look good.

But she'd never expected to look like *this* . . .

Chapter Four

As the light from outside fell over Olivia, Ivy's jaw dropped.

I know that dress!

Sleek, black, and mysterious, it was the goth gown Amelia had designed for Ivy . . . which meant that *she* must be wearing the super-bunnified dress that Penny had designed for Olivia!

'Stupid broken lights!' Ivy groaned.

'What was that?' Amelia swung around sharply. 'Is something wrong?'

'Never mind,' Ivy mumbled. She'd just have to brave this through – the last thing she needed right now was for the Goth-Queen to have a meltdown!

But I never thought I'd have to walk that runway in front of everybody while wearing pink . . . or is it blue? She couldn't even remember – she hadn't paid enough attention to Olivia's gown at dress rehearsal. *Whatever it is, it's definitely not goth!*

'Go! Go!' Penny shooed her through.

Ivy tried to smile as she stepped out into the hot, bright spotlights. She had a horrible feeling, though, that her 'modelling smile' was coming off more like a sickly grimace . . . especially after she took a quick, desperate look at what she was wearing.

If only this spotlight was sunlight and I was *a movie vampire!* Right now, spontaneous combustion sounded *so* much better than half-walking, half-strutting towards the runway in Olivia's frilly blue-and-white dress!

Her smile faltered as she stepped up on to

the runway and heard the audience gasp. The contrast between her and her goth-outfitted sister, on the other side of the catwalk, must have been absolutely stunning . . . and it made her want to burst into sky-high flames just to escape!

Olivia's perfect movie-star/model's smile never faltered, but as they passed each other on the runway, she mumbled out of the corner of her mouth: 'Sorry!'

Me, too, Ivy thought. She bit back a sigh as she took in her sister's appearance.

Olivia, of course, looked as fabulous as always – but hadn't anyone ever told her that goths didn't *do* delighted grins in public?

But then, bunnies aren't supposed to do scowls, either, she told herself. With an effort, she tried to notch up her own smile. *At least one of us should match her dress tonight!*

Walking all four points on the x-shaped runway seemed to take forever, with humiliation burning through her at every step . . . but finally, finally, she was finished. Ivy nearly ran down the steps on the far side to join the other models who had congregated there.

'And now,' Lillian announced behind her, 'our final model, presenting the young designers' stunning new collaboration: "Altegular"!'

Even Ivy turned around for that.

Reiko's blood-red hair gleamed in the spotlight . . . but nothing could take the focus away from her stunning dress. There was no whispering this time from the audience – only a stunned silence as they took in the half-black, half-pink gown, with embroidered clasped hands running along the seams – and Tessa's deep red pashmina cleverly arranged above it all.

I bet no one in the audience has ever seen anything like it before, Ivy thought. She sure hadn't . . . but she knew exactly what the design of the dress meant, and she couldn't help the tiny smile that curved her lips as she took it in.

Together, Penny and Amelia had designed the perfect symbol of how Franklin Grove High had changed for the better in the past few weeks. Goths and bunnies had once been totally separate, but now those barriers were broken down – and a lot of that was down to Penny and Amelia.

I don't usually care much about fashion, Ivy thought, *but this is actually kind of genius.* The choice to accessorise that dress with the priceless pashmina was alternative *and* mainstream, both at once.

Perfectly Altegular!

Reiko strutted proudly down the runway as the stunned silence was gradually broken by more and more murmurs of appreciation . . . and then a swell of growing applause! As the cheers rose higher and higher around the runway, Ivy felt her shoulders relax and an actual smile break across her face for the first time in hours.

'Ohh . . .!' Olivia's own grin made her positively glow in the slinky goth gown. 'Can you believe how great this is?'

Ivy shrugged, still smiling. 'I guess they were right not to give any previews or hints about this one, huh?'

'Absolutely.' Olivia's eyes never wavered from Reiko, who had struck a fabulous pose to soak in the applause like a true model. 'This was just the right way to do it.'

Flashbulbs clicked across the room as the gathered audience raced to snap photos before Reiko could end her turn onstage. As Ivy's vampire hearing took in all the murmurs around the room, she had to admit . . .

Maybe this fashion show hadn't been such a bad idea after all.

Ivy shuddered. *Between this bunnified dress and that scary thought, even I don't know who I am any more!*

🦇 🦇 🦇

Fifteen minutes later, Ivy was feeling even better, with the spotlights finally turned off and the runway dismantled to let the guests flood all the way into the room. She might still have been wearing 'the blue horror', as she'd privately renamed her gown, but now that she was standing to one side with Olivia and their bio-dad, no one's eyes were on her any more. *Thank darkness!*

Better yet, Charles looked absolutely giddy with pride in his wife, whose opening night had been truly spectacular. 'You were both wonderful,' he said, putting his hands on their shoulders. 'And Olivia?' he turned to Ivy.

Ivy sighed. *Great, I'm a bunny.*

'That's Ivy, Dad!' cried Olivia. 'We put the wrong dresses on by mistake. I can't believe you couldn't tell!'

Charles' eyes widened as he stared at his daughters and then he burst out laughing, 'Well, I was wondering why Ivy was smiling so much but that explains it! Anyway,' he said, turning to the real Olivia, 'I'm very pleased that I let you talk me into using the Vein of Love as part of the fashion show.'

Ivy blinked. 'Um . . . should I be grossed out?'

Charles laughed. 'No, no, it's only Tessa's pashmina,' he explained. 'It was used at her wedding to fulfil a ritual that's commonly known as the "Vein of Love". Other weddings have used a red scarf or a length of red velvet or silk, but Alex and Tessa's pashmina worked perfectly for the ritual.'

'Seriously?' Ivy traded a wide-eyed glance with Olivia. 'We were at that wedding, but I don't remember any . . . "*rituals*".'

'No?' Charles raised his eyebrows, his voice taking on a lecturing tone. 'Tessa's pashmina symbolises the deep bond between a prince and princess. Don't you remember, at the wedding reception, the moment when Alex and Tessa danced while each holding on to one end of the pashmina?'

'Ohhh,' Olivia breathed. '*That* was a ritual? I thought it was just a dance.'

'It wasn't just a dance,' Charles told her. 'It was also an ancient, Transylvanian tradition.' He smiled faintly, dropping his voice to a whisper. 'It symbolised that their love is "everlasting" . . . *immortal*.'

'Got it,' Ivy murmured.

'But . . .' Olivia looked a little queasy. 'Why does it have to be the *Vein* of Love? I mean, are vamps so committed to darkness, they have to make even romance feel just a little bit . . . *bleurgh*?'

'Ah, now there's the downside.' Charles shook his head ominously. 'If the Vein of Love is ever broken – ruined or damaged – the marriage it once blessed is doomed to fail!'

'Yeah, right.' Ivy scoffed. 'I don't see *that* happening, do you?'

Olivia laughed. 'Even if that superstition was true, there would be *no* chance of it happening with Alex and Tessa! I've never seen any couple so in love.'

'And speaking of *seeing* . . .' Ivy winced as she glanced down at her frilly white sleeves. 'We need to go get out of these dresses before I turn permanently bunnified!'

Laughing, they stepped together into the still-darkened changing room. Someone had finally got hold of a torch, and by the light of its glow, they could see Amelia and Penny stroking the pashmina fondly as it lay folded over Penny's arm.

'I hate to say goodbye to it,' Penny said wistfully.

'It was definitely the star of the show!' Amelia agreed.

'Oh, I don't know.' Reiko's voice rang out cheekily from the darkness beyond. 'It would have been nothing without me!'

Grinning, Ivy rolled her eyes. At least it was good to see that the exchange student had finally recovered from the shock of riding in Jackson Caulfield's limousine tonight!

'Do you want me to take the pashmina back to its display for you, as soon as I've changed?' Ivy asked Amelia and Penny. 'That way, you guys can go mingle and meet everyone.'

'You really should,' Olivia agreed immediately. 'There are so many people out there waiting to meet the designers!'

'Thank you!' Amelia gave the pashmina one last stroke, then stepped away. 'And thanks again for taking part tonight, you guys.'

'Actually . . .' Penny held the pashmina over her arm, biting her lip. 'If you don't mind, Ivy, I'll come with you. I haven't seen much of the museum yet – and, this way, I can put off saying goodbye to the pashmina for another couple of minutes!'

Ivy shook her head as she began to change. *Never again!* she promised herself. Putting on her own slinky black gown felt like coming home. She felt like a brand-new 'Old Ivy' five minutes later as she set off with Penny through the halls of the museum.

When she flicked on the lights of the display room where her dad kept the pashmina, as part of his Transylvanian history exhibit, Penny gasped.

'Ohhh! I was in such a hurry earlier to get the pashmina, I barely noticed the rest of these! All of them are so gorgeous, I almost wish I had a time machine!'

'Really?' Ivy wrinkled her nose as she looked at the rich costumes arranged around them, from cloaks to tunics and long, flowing gowns. 'I don't see what's so great about them.'

Ivy let her friend geek out over the old fashions while she turned to put the pashmina back in its case. The rich red silk felt soft against her hands as she arranged it on its velvet hanger.

'Olivia was right,' she whispered to it. 'Who would call something so gorgeous the "Vein of Love"? Yuck!'

She stepped back and closed the glass display case, before heading out of the room.

'I'm *definitely* coming back again tomorrow to get some new design ideas!' Penny started after Ivy . . . just as the lights flickered and went out.

'Not this room, too!' Ivy groaned. 'Dad had better get on to somebody about this, or it's really going to affect museum business. If they don't get it fixed –'

A loud clatter sounded behind her, cutting her off.

'Penny?' Ivy spun around. 'Are you OK? Did you crash into something?'

'It wasn't me,' Penny said. Her voice came from just behind Ivy, sounding suddenly strained.

'Is there someone else in here?'

Suddenly, Ivy's skin felt too tight. With her ears pricked for any sound, she heard every breath in the room . . . including that of a third person, only feet away in the darkness . . .

Someone else is *in here*, Ivy thought, a shudder running through her. Then she grimaced.

I'm scared of a stranger in the dark. I have to be the worst vampire in the world!

'Hey!' she yelled, forcing anger into her voice, above the fear. 'Whoever's there, stop creeping around right now. It's not funny, it's just stupid!'

Shuffling noises sounded against the tiled floor on the other side of the room.

The lights came back on with a flash. Ivy blinked against the sudden glare, spun around . . .

. . . and found no one. Penny stood just behind her, eyes wide and panicked, but they were the only ones in the big, echoing room.

'I don't understand,' Penny whispered. 'I could

have sworn I heard someone.'

'I *know* I heard someone,' Ivy said grimly. 'Whoever it was, though, they must have taken their chance to disappear before the lights turned back on.'

'Oh!' Penny's gasp sounded almost like a scream. 'Ivy . . .' She pointed, her finger quivering. '*Look!*'

Feeling heavy with dread, Ivy turned . . .

'Oh, no,' she whispered.

The intruder wasn't the only thing that had disappeared.

The display case she'd closed only a few moments ago hung open . . . and the velvet hanger was empty.

Tessa's priceless pashmina had been stolen!

Ivy staggered, reaching out for something, *anything*, to catch herself on before she could faint.

'Ivy!' Penny grabbed her arm to steady her. 'Are you OK?'

'No.' Ivy's voice cracked as she imagined her dad's reaction to the news . . . and worse yet, how Alex and Tessa would feel when they found out their 'Vein of Love' had been stolen.

In every possible way, tonight had been a total *fashion frightmare*!

Chapter Five

In her bio-dad's house the next morning, Olivia fumbled her way down the black-carpeted staircase, yawning and stretching. *Worry does not make for good sleep!*

After Ivy had told her about the theft, it had been impossible to drop off . . . and the fact that she'd heard Ivy tossing and turning all night long in her coffin across the room hadn't made it any easier! Olivia loved her vampire sister, but it was still seriously spooky to hear the thumps and thuds of a body knocking around inside a coffin, in the dark. *Talk about nightmares . . .*

Still yawning, Olivia walked towards the

kitchen and found Ivy and Charles at the table already. Ivy had a full bowl of Marshmallow Platelets sitting, ignored, in front of her as she slumped in her chair, rubbing her elbow.

'I think my coffin needs a new lining!'

'I'll take a look at it later,' Charles promised, not looking up from the newspaper on his lap. 'Ah, Olivia!' As she stepped through the doorway, he smiled and pointed to a manila envelope that was on the worktop. 'That was dropped off for you by a courier first thing.'

'For me? Who would send it to me *here*?' She'd only spent the night in Ivy's house as a special treat, to celebrate Café Creative's opening night. Frowning, Olivia reached out to pick up the envelope . . . then relaxed as she recognised the handwriting on the back.

'Jackson?' Ivy asked from the table.

'Yeah.' Smiling, Olivia sank down into an empty seat and opened the envelope as Charles returned to his newspaper, humming a tune that sounded like it might have come from some opera a hundred years ago or more. Knowing Charles, it probably had!

A thick sheaf of typescript slipped out of the envelope, along with a handwritten note:

These are the revised pages for the scenes we'll be shooting in Pine Wood next month. I had to catch a six a.m. flight to get to that hospital visit in Chicago, but I'll be in touch as soon as I land. I miss you already!

A stab of regret pierced Olivia as she set down the note. It would be so many weeks before she'd see him again . . . but she felt a warm pride, too. Jackson was giving up his own free time to visit some of his youngest fans in hospital . . . and as much as she might miss him now, the fact that he would do something like that was a big part of why she loved him.

'I can't believe you're smiling right now!' Ivy hissed. 'Do you even remember what happened?'

Oops! Olivia sighed. She hadn't even realised she was smiling. *Talk about inappropriate!*

But this was all *so* unfair. She and Ivy should have been basking in the success of the Café's grand opening this morning. Most of the town *was* buzzing about it, judging from the texts Olivia had gotten from friends all through the night! But the theft had cast a shadow – a shadow that only Olivia and Ivy could see.

As she stood up to pour some cereal and orange juice for herself, she shot a quick look at Charles. He was still humming happily over his copy of *The Franklin Grove Reporter*, and no wonder: the front cover showed a giant photo of Reiko in last night's fashion show . . . wearing the pashmina that had been stolen less than an hour later.

Suddenly, she didn't feel hungry any more. And she knew Charles would not be humming if he only knew the truth of what had happened last night.

If the twins couldn't find the pashmina themselves, they would definitely have to tell their bio-dad and stepmom . . . but there was no question about it: Charles and Lillian would both totally panic. It would be enough of a nightmare for *any* of the museum's treasures to be stolen – but Tessa's pashmina, with all those vamp superstitions surrounding it? *That's a whole new level of disaster!*

Olivia tried hard to sound casual as she cleared her throat. 'So, Dad . . . what more can you tell me about the' – *yuck!* – '. . . Vein of Love?'

Ivy gave a nervous twitch that sent Marsh-mallow Platelets flying off her spoon.

Luckily, Charles – his attention still focused on the newspaper – didn't seem to notice. 'Oh, the origins of that tradition are so obscure, even vampires argue about the precise dates,' he murmured. 'So, imagine how *long ago* the tradition must have begun!'

'Right,' Ivy muttered, looking green. 'Just imagine.'

And now we've ruined it. Olivia set down her spoon and swallowed hard.

The timer on the oven dinged loudly, and Charles's head jerked up. 'Aha!' Smiling broadly, he tucked the newspaper under his arm and hurried to the oven. 'After all her hard work, I thought I'd give Lillian a celebratory breakfast-in-dead this morning!'

Olivia's mouth fell open.

'Don't worry,' Ivy mumbled through her mouthful of cereal. 'It's just the vamp equivalent of breakfast-in-bed.'

'Indeed.' Humming the thumping runway music from the night before, Charles scooped up the food and headed for the door. 'I'll be right back!'

When the twins were sure he was upstairs, Ivy sagged back in her chair. 'I can't believe this . . . *What* are we going to do?'

'We have to tell the police,' Olivia said. 'It's our only choice.'

'No way!' Ivy held her spoon as if it were a weapon. 'This is a vampire issue. We need to deal with it ourselves. Besides, the police won't exactly go into overdrive just to find a stolen pashmina, will they?'

'Maybe you're right,' Olivia sighed. 'But what about Prince Alex and Tessa? They're supposed to be spending today in Adamstown, half an hour away from here. Don't you think we should tell them first, so they can join in the search?'

'Absolutely not.' Ivy leaned forward, setting her arms on the table. Her eyes were narrowed with concentration, her investigative brain obviously hard at work. 'I don't think we should tell Alex and Tessa anything unless they specifically ask about it.'

'Right,' Olivia nodded. 'We don't want to get Amelia and Penny into trouble.'

'Of course not.' Ivy shook her head. 'Plus, it would totally ruin Alex and Tessa's trip. We don't want them to freak out about bad luck.'

Olivia winced. As wonderful as Alex and Tessa were, they were Transylvanian vampires to the core – which meant, they were intensely superstitious! 'You're right.' She took a deep breath. 'So, where do we start?'

Ivy made a rueful face. 'Honestly? I have *no* idea. But this is the most important mystery we've ever been faced with.'

Olivia grinned at her. 'We are the Daring Detective Duo,' Olivia said. 'Come on. Let's go to work!'

They marched together out of the kitchen towards the stairs, leaving the uneaten cereal bowls behind them . . .

And the doorbell rang loudly.

Olivia traded a quick, panicked look with Ivy as they both froze at the bottom of the stairs.

Had Alex and Tessa found out somehow about the theft? What if they were here to demand answers?

Olivia hurried after her sister to the front door. Squaring her shoulders, Ivy swung it open . . .

Reiko beamed at them both from the doorstep. She looked as fresh and well-rested as if she'd slept for days, and her hair was coloured such a bright green, Olivia actually had to take a step back.

'Hi!' Reiko bounced on the toes of her tennis shoes, looking at the twins expectantly. 'Are you two ready for school?'

'What?' Olivia frowned, confused.

'Oh, *no.*' Ivy groaned and fell back against the doorway. 'I can't believe it. I was so focused, I actually forgot I'm still a fourteen-year-old girl who has to go to *school*!'

'Huh?' Reiko looked between the two of them, frowning. 'I don't understand.'

'I'll explain later.' Ivy sighed. 'Come on, Olivia. We'll have to wait until after school to start investigating.'

'Maybe.' Olivia glanced at the clock on the wall – then down at her pyjamas. She winced. 'But only if the Daring Detective Duo don't get an after-school detention for tardiness!'

She gave Reiko a quick, apologetic smile – *Explanations will have to wait!* – then hurried upstairs, leaving the green-haired exchange student behind.

Four hours later, Ivy scowled down at her school lunch. Thank darkness she wasn't dealing with Amelia-levels of popularity any more, and could trust that her expression was enough to keep her cafeteria table clear of unwanted guests.

It wasn't that she disliked the other students at her school – it was just that, with the mystery of the missing pashmina circling over and over again through her head, she needed all the thinking time she could get. Right now, there was only one thing she could be sure of: the pashmina had been on display not as a "vampire" artefact, but rather as a *Transylvanian* one. That meant that the thief was *probably* not someone who was actually aiming to bring bad luck to Alex and Tessa, because the thief *probably* did not know the vampire secret. Instead, it was more likely to have been just an opportunistic bunny who had seen it, liked it, and wanted it for themselves.

But how am I supposed to get into the head of someone like that?

She gave a frustrated sigh. If it had been a vampire, she might have been able to think like them and figure out where they would hide it. But a human thief, who had stolen something just because they wanted it . . .

I will just never understand humans, Ivy thought glumly. They might look like vampires, but sometimes it felt like they were an alien species! And if she couldn't figure out what had brought the thief to the museum in the first place . . .

Her breath caught. There *was* something she knew about her mysterious thief, wasn't there?

It has to be someone our age.

The realisation felt like a bell going off in the back of her brain. The audience for the fashion show had been almost completely made up of teenagers – mostly from Franklin Grove High, who'd come specifically to see Amelia's and Penny's designs. That meant the thief could actually be someone Ivy knew.

They could be in the cafeteria right now, she thought. *I could sit next to them in a class, or –*

'Hey!' Fingers snapped in her face, and Ivy jerked upright, blinking hard.

Her table wasn't empty any more. As her vision cleared, she found Reiko and Olivia sitting across from her . . . and from the dent in Olivia's veggie burger, they'd been there for a few minutes.

'Sorry!' Ivy mumbled. She could feel her cheeks paling with embarrassment. 'I was miles away.'

'We could tell.' Olivia gave her a concerned look. 'Have you had any brilliant detecting ideas yet?'

Ivy shook her head. 'None at all.'

'Oh.' Olivia slumped.

The fraught silence between the sisters was broken by a weary sigh from Reiko, who'd heard the whole story on the way to school that morning. 'You know, in Japan we hear stories about the Euro-American banps and all their tradition and drama.' She frowned. 'I always thought it sounded fun – but actually, it's just making me feel a little tense!'

'Tell me about it,' Ivy mumbled.

'Ivy!' Amelia's voice hissed just behind her. 'We need to talk!'

Ivy turned around. For once, the Goth-

101

Queen's thick black hair looked uncombed, and her chalk-white make-up was smudged. Next to Amelia, Penny carried a long, thin box in her arms and looked as pale as if she'd reverted back to her old goth self . . . but her pallor didn't come from make-up. Instead, Penny just looked dead tired.

'Have you heard anything about the pashmina?' Amelia muttered, her eyes darting around the room, as if she was watching out for eavesdroppers.

Ivy shrugged unhappily. 'It's still gone.'

Amelia sagged. Suddenly, her leather jacket looked too big on her.

'We still feel terrible about what happened,' Penny whispered. 'But . . .'

Taking a deep breath, she leaned over the table to set down the box. Ivy, Olivia and Reiko all crowded round to watch as Penny opened it . . .

. . . and Ivy let out an actual squeak as she saw

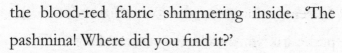

the blood-red fabric shimmering inside. 'The pashmina! Where did you find it?'

'Nowhere,' Amelia sighed.

'What do you mean?' Ivy couldn't look away from the beautiful silk. Reverently, she reached out to stroke it. 'I don't understand.'

'This is just a replica,' said Penny. 'We stayed up all night making it, so that it can go on display in the museum while we all search for the original one.'

'Oh.' Ivy's hand dropped away. Disappointment tasted so bitter in her mouth, she had to fight not to let out a groan of frustration.

'It really is a wonderful replica,' Olivia said softly. 'I could never tell the difference.'

'Me neither,' Reiko said. 'And I wore the real thing last night!'

'It's great,' Ivy said. 'Really. Thank you.' She forced a smile for the two designers. 'You created the perfect replacement.'

Penny brightened. 'We hand-dyed the pashmina to match the exact shade of red. It's not *completely* perfect, but the untrained eye shouldn't notice a thing.'

What about untrained vampire *eyes?* Ivy wondered. She peered harder . . . but no. She definitely couldn't tell the difference, vampire vision or no.

'Whew.' Ivy sighed. 'At least there won't be any drama at the museum if no one even realises the pashmina is missing.'

'But we still have to find the real one,' Olivia finished quietly.

Ivy nodded unhappily.

It was the worst possible moment to look up and see Brendan approaching the table with the world's most inappropriate grin. He was still snickering as he slid into the seat beside Ivy.

'What could *possibly* be so funny?' Ivy snapped. He knew the truth about the pashmina; she'd confided in him last night. *Doesn't he even realise we're dealing with a disaster?*

'Oh . . . nothing,' Brendan drawled, sliding her a mischievous sideways glance.

'Seriously!' She pinched his forearm. 'What *is* it?'

'I don't think I can explain it with words,' Brendan said solemnly. He reached into his pocket and took out his smartphone. 'I think . . . you have to *see* this one for yourself!'

He pressed a button to illuminate the screen.

Ivy sucked in a gasp. 'What . . .?'

It was a picture of her, wearing a fabulous goth gown – and smiling like she'd just been handed free front-row tickets for a Pall Bearers concert.

'I've never smiled that widely in my life!'

'You didn't,' Olivia said, biting her bottom lip. 'That's a picture from last night . . .'

'So it's actually *you* . . .' Ivy shook her head in wonder. 'Wow. Even I couldn't tell the difference.'

'No one else can, either. Everyone who's seen this picture thinks it's you. And that's not all . . .' Brendan gave an evil chuckle as he swiped his finger across the screen. This time, he brought up the same picture – but with red-and-white lettering under 'Ivy's' smiling face. It read: 'Shadowtown *is back on the air . . . Woo-hoo!*'

'What on earth?' Ivy whispered.

Brendan swiped his finger across the screen again. This time, the picture came up with the phrase: *'I can't believe it – black goes with black!'* One more swipe, and a third version came up: *'What are you talking about? This is my "solemn" face.'*

Ivy's head almost fell into her burger. 'I've gone viral?!'

'I doubt it, sweetie,' Amelia said decisively, looking over her shoulder. 'I haven't seen this photo anywhere.'

'I haven't seen it either!' Penny added. 'That means it can't be all over the internet.'

106

'Um . . .' Biting her lip, Ivy shared a look with Brendan.

The photo might not be up anywhere on the *bunny* internet . . . but that didn't mean it wasn't taking the Vorld Vide Veb by storm! And if there was one thing all vamps found hilarious, it was the idea of 'happy', smiley vampires.

This could be the beginning of something very, very irritating, Ivy realised glumly.

She might actually wear out her death-squint if this went on!

There was no time to worry about that now. *First things first.* She had to reclaim the Vein of Love as soon as possible, no matter what that took.

After that's taken care of, then *I'm definitely going to put a stake in this viral photo!*

Chapter Six

The moment that school finally finished for the day, Olivia headed towards the museum with Ivy and Reiko. It was closed to the public until the weekend, while staff cleared up after Café Creative's opening night, but Olivia and Ivy had begged their bio-dad for a private visit.

Charles might be firm when he came to his work – but he couldn't fight his enthusiasm for the past. And Olivia had used all her acting skills to persuade him of how desperate she was to see the artefacts under less stressful circumstances . . .

Which isn't actually a lie, Olivia reassured herself

now. After all, she really did want to take her time with the artefacts – soon. Today, she had a slightly more important goal!

Officially, they were on their way to get a special tour from Charles . . . but *un*officially, Olivia and Ivy were on a secret mission to put the fake pashmina in place. Olivia knew Ivy was planning to practise her investigative journalism skills this afternoon, by snooping around for any trail the thief might have left for them to follow.

Speeding up, Olivia overtook Ivy and Reiko to turn the final corner on the way to the museum . . .

. . . and came to a dead halt as she saw the couple coming straight towards them.

'Alex! Tessa!' Olivia squeaked. 'How . . . *nice* to see you again.'

Behind her, Ivy let out a muffled groan. Even Reiko lost her athletic balance for once as she hid herself behind Olivia.

'Prince!' she mumbled, clutching at Olivia's arms, her voice sounding strangled with panic. 'Prince . . . Princess . . . *Ack!*'

Alex frowned, setting one hand on his wife's back, as Ivy caught Olivia just in time. 'Are you girls OK?'

'Yes!' Olivia said, disentangling herself from Reiko. 'We're great. Totally great. And you two look . . . great!' *Great?* She squeezed her eyes shut for a moment, wincing. *Could I sound any less convincing?*

Every inch of her was aware of the decoy pashmina in Ivy's bag. It was as if it was shooting out radio signals into the air that screamed: *'Fake! They're trying to pass off a fake!'*

Taking a long, deep breath, she opened her eyes again . . . and frowned. *Wait a minute.*

Alex and Tessa did *not* look great at all. In fact, they looked a little . . .

Spooked, she realised. *Uh-oh*. She tried not to

glance in the direction of Ivy's bag. She could almost hear the fake pashmina shouting into the air:

'Don't trust these girls! I'm not your real pashmina!'

No. Taking hold of herself, Olivia forced the vision aside. *There's no reason they should know about the theft.*

'Are *you* OK?' Ivy asked the royal couple.

Alex and Tessa traded a look, and Olivia's concern deepened. Forgetting the pashmina, she started forward. 'Something *is* wrong,' she said firmly. 'Please tell us.'

'Well . . .' Alex sighed, holding Tessa protectively. 'The truth is . . . our day in Adamstown was not exactly fun.'

Tessa sighed. 'It's true. First, my dress got caught in the doors of the train that took us there – and if I hadn't had vampire strength, I would have been dragged with it all the way along the platform!'

Olivia gasped. 'That's terrible!'

Tessa held up the torn skirt of her long, elegant dark green dress. 'Just look at it! This was my favourite dress.'

'It's . . . still beautiful,' Reiko mumbled, with an obvious effort. The words were kind, but from the look on her face, it gave her actual physical pain to speak to such a celebrity.

'At least Tessa wasn't hurt,' Alex said. 'But then things got even worse.' Looking miserable, he clamped his mouth shut.

'Well?' Ivy prompted. 'What happened next?'

Tessa patted Alex's arm soothingly. 'The restaurant we had lunch at served us *medium-rare* steaks.' She winced. 'Alex almost broke through the wall to get to the restroom.'

'Ouch!' said Ivy.

Reiko made a sympathetic face. 'I *hate* it when that happens!'

Poor Alex! Olivia thought, seeing the usually

dashing prince looking mortified – quietly and stoically mortified, of course, but still mortified.

'Anyway,' he mumbled, 'we thought it was time to give up on our day out. So we –'

Caw! Caw!

Out of nowhere, a crow appeared in the air above them. As Olivia stared in shock, it dived down to flap crazily around Alex and Tessa's heads.

The newlyweds ducked, throwing up their arms in self-defence.

'Shoo!' Ivy yelled, starting forward and waving her arms. 'Go away!'

But the bird followed after Alex and Tessa, cawing louder. They both spun to try to escape it – and Alex's leg caught in Tessa's torn skirt. Her arm windmilled as she searched for balance . . . and their heads crashed straight into each other.

The royal couple fell to the ground in a

tangled heap, while the bird wheeled away with one last *caw*!

'Are you OK?' Striding forward gracefully, Reiko reached them first.

Ivy and Olivia were right behind her, all of them helping the stunned couple to their feet. As Tessa dusted down her dress, she gave a shaky laugh.

'If I didn't know better,' she said, 'I'd think this trip was cursed!'

Oh, no. Olivia didn't dare look at Ivy . . . or the bag with the fake pashmina inside.

'You're probably just imagining it,' Ivy said. Her voice sounded strangled.

'It's true,' Olivia added quickly. 'Jet-lag can do weird things to people. Trust me – I've been flying around so much these last few months, I'm not entirely sure this isn't just a really strange dream!'

Ivy gave an unconvincing chuckle. 'That would make it your fault I'm living a hell as a

Vorld-Vide-Veb-joke, huh?'

Alex clapped one hand over his mouth, but his snicker escaped anyway. Tessa let out a muffled snort.

'Oh, no . . .' Ivy stared at them. 'Are you telling me that even *you guys* have seen it?'

'Um . . .' Tessa pressed her lips together, but her eyes were sparkling with suppressed laughter.

'Well,' Alex said, 'I wouldn't say we've seen *all* the different versions online yet . . .'

'But there are so many,' Tessa said apologetically, 'they're just very hard to miss!'

'And there are some really *good* ones,' Alex added. His grin broke through as he dug his smartphone out of his pocket. 'Here, I bookmarked my favourite.' He held out the phone, and Olivia, Reiko and Ivy peered at it together.

Yet again, they looked at 'Ivy's' beaming face above her goth gown . . . and this time, the

caption read: *'Half-price Marshmallow Platelets . . .
Oh yeah!'*

Ivy groaned. 'I can't take many more of these!'

'OK.' Still smiling, Alex slid the phone back
into his pocket. 'But anyway . . . if you guys
are going to the museum, maybe we could tag
along?'

'Oh, yes!' Tessa nodded enthusiastically. 'We
need to do *something* fun to improve the day. And
I'd love to see my pashmina hanging up there!'

Uh-oh. Olivia felt Ivy's arm stiffen under
her hand. She thought fast. 'Erm . . . we're not
actually going to the museum right now.'

'Really?' Alex blinked, looking from Olivia to
the museum's front door, only fifteen feet away.
'But –'

'It's locked up!' Ivy said hastily. 'Until this
weekend. And Albert would *never* let us in out-of-
hours!'

Tessa frowned. 'Who's Albert?'

116

'The caretaker,' Olivia explained. 'You must have seen him last night, or when you visited the museum before. You know, the vampire who always wears jogging outfits?'

'Sorry,' said Ivy, doing her best sad-face. 'The museum is definitely off-limits today.'

'Oh, that's right, I just remembered!' Reiko chimed in. 'Perhaps we should go and catch a game instead?'

Ivy looked like she was preparing her death-squint, so Olivia stepped in. 'I think we could all do with something to eat.' She clapped her hands decisively. 'Come on. Let's go to . . . Mister Smoothie's!'

Ivy's death-squint was immediately turned on Olivia, but she ignored it.

'Mister . . . Smoothie's?' Tessa's brow crinkled in a frown. 'Is that some kind of café?'

'You'll love it,' Olivia told her, trying to sound breezy. *And it's on the other side of town — far away*

117

from the museum. 'It's just what you need to turn your day around.'

Why could I only think of Mister Smoothie's? It's like a vampire's worst nightmare! She didn't need Ivy's glare to tell her this was a bad idea . . .

Chapter Seven

*W*ell, *I* knew *that was a bad idea* . . .

As Ivy pulled on her backpack the next morning, she sniffed the ends of her long hair – and groaned. *Yup.* She could still smell the peach-and-blood-orange smoothie. *It just won't go away!* Even two rounds of shampoo last night hadn't been enough to remove the evidence of yesterday's . . . *incident.*

I don't care how much the bunnies like them, smoothies are dangerous!

Olivia had spent the whole journey there telling Alex and Tessa exactly how delicious their smoothies would be. By the time they'd arrived,

Tessa really seemed to have forgotten how excited she'd been about the museum. And – typically for Transylvanian vamps! – she and Alex had taken the business of ordering *very* seriously. It had taken ages for them both to select exactly the right flavours.

Unfortunately, when the Mister Smoothie's clerk was putting those two particular orders on to the counter, she lost her balance and had somehow managed to drop them . . . *upwards*!

The cups had arced and fallen, peach and raspberry and blueberry smoothie mingling into a crazy rainbow . . . and with a line of customers waiting behind them, there had been no way for Tessa or Alex to escape.

The entire group had been splashed.

Ivy recalled the horror on the shop clerk's face as she'd stared at the sopping wet, smoothie-covered prince and princess, offering apologies, free replacements . . . and lots of towels.

She couldn't have been more obviously sincere, but when Tessa had told her it was OK, Ivy had definitely detected a note of panic in the princess's voice.

Tessa might be one of the most easy-going people Ivy knew, but it was obvious that her string of bad luck was starting to seriously rattle her. *If she finds out that the pashmina's been stolen, she might just have a nervous breakdown!*

Ivy had to track down the thief before that could happen.

Sighing, she headed out the front door towards the bus stop on Undertaker Hill. Reiko was already waiting there, her hair dyed in contrasting streaks of black and white, matching the soccer ball she was juggling between her feet and knees.

'Wow.' Ivy shook her head in disbelief as she joined the exchange student. 'Did you actually buy that just for the next week and a half?'

Still juggling the ball, Reiko gave a shrug. 'I was bored.'

'Bored?!' Ivy repeated. 'You've won doubles tennis and starred in a fashion show. Now we're dealing with a stolen treasure, a thief to hunt, *and* a string of terrible luck for Alex and Tessa! How much more drama do you need?'

'Well . . .' Reiko looked thoughtful, as the bus chugged down the street towards them. 'I still haven't made it to a real sports game.'

Unbelievable. Shaking her head, Ivy stepped on to the school bus without another word.

❥ ❥ ❥

The second they stepped out of the bus at Franklin Grove High, Reiko's soccer ball was back in action, bouncing off her knees and feet in a stream of constant motion. Bunnies and goths alike stopped to stare as they passed, the constant *thump-thump-thump* hammering into Ivy's skull as they walked into the building.

Does she ever stop? Ivy gritted her teeth. *Pretend it isn't happening,* she ordered herself . . . but she couldn't do it. She couldn't even look away from the rocketing soccer ball until –

'Hey! Watch out!' A goth senior stepped back, rubbing his shoulder where Ivy had just crashed into him.

'Sorry,' she mumbled. She forced herself to turn her gaze ahead, but all she could focus on was the soccer ball bouncing in the corner of her vision. At any minute, it was definitely going to hit someone, or –

'Ow!' A hefty, muscled football player let out a yelp of pain as Ivy's shoulder banged into his arm. He backed away, massaging it. 'Watch where you're going!'

Great. Now I'm *the menace in this hallway!*

Blowing out her breath in frustration, Ivy came to a halt in front of her locker; beside her, Reiko still juggled the ball. It bounced off the closest locker again and again, with a dull metallic clang each time. *Thump-bang! Thump-bang! Thump-bang!*

Ivy started to reach into her locker for her textbooks – then stopped. *I can't even remember which classes I have this morning! This is crazy.* Taking a deep breath, she closed her eyes and tried to focus. OK, today was a Friday, and that meant . . .

Thump-bang!

That meant her first-period class should be –

Thump-bang!

'Oh, for darkness' sake!' Ivy spun around, her eyes flaring wide open. 'Can you *please* just stop that for *five seconds* to let me think?'

Reiko caught the ball in her hands, the shock on her face making guilt surge through Ivy.

'Is something wrong?' Reiko asked.

'It's . . .' Ivy sighed, fighting back her frustration. 'It's just, the sound of that ball over and *over* again . . . well, it's starting to get to me

124

a little bit. I've got a lot on my mind.'

'Sorry.' Reiko shrugged, jiggling the ball in her hands. 'This is just how I get when I have energy to burn off.'

'You have energy to "burn off"?' Ivy let out a half-laugh of disbelief. She lowered her voice to a whisper as she pulled out her English textbook from her locker. 'It's first-thing on a Friday. Most vamps our age are so tired right now they can't wait to get back to their coffins and go to sleep again. And considering you haven't stayed still for a single second since you got here –'

'Well . . .' Reiko blinked, stepping back an inch. 'I don't mean to annoy anybody with my energy, but . . . I told you, I'm kind of bored. This trip hasn't been quite what I was hoping for.' She shrugged. 'You haven't exactly been the most enthusiastic of hostesses . . .'

'Are you kidding?' Ivy slammed her locker shut. 'Have you not noticed that I have a bit of a crisis going on? I'm sorry if I haven't played as much tennis or soccer as you would have liked, but we do have a few more important issues to worry about!'

Reiko shrugged and spun the soccer ball on one finger. 'You do remember you're a teenager, right? Occasionally, it is OK for you to do what *you* think would be fun.'

'Well, that would never involve sports,' Ivy snapped.

Reiko's eyebrows shot upwards. She closed her mouth tightly as she caught the soccer ball.

Silence grew between them . . . and Ivy heard her own words repeated in an endless, horrible loop in her head. Shame swept in a hot wave through her body, making her skin burn. 'I'm sorry,' she mumbled. 'I didn't mean –'

'Forget it.' Reiko tucked the ball under her arm. Suddenly, she looked as subdued and serious as Ivy could ever have wished . . . and she turned away without meeting Ivy's gaze. 'I'll see you in class,' she said.

She set off in the direction of their English class, leaving Ivy staring miserably after her and wondering how she could have made things so much *worse*.

Only the sound of her cell phone beeping in her backpack forced her to look away from Reiko's retreating back. Sighing, Ivy pulled out the phone.

It was a text from Sophia: *So, how is the Queen of the Vorld Vide Veb doing? I think I'm missing all the fun!*

Ha. Ivy shook her head as she tucked the phone back into her backpack.

Sophia might be missing home, but right now she certainly wasn't missing any 'fun'!

Ivy slung her backpack over her shoulder and started for class with heavy feet. When she walked into the room, she came to a dead halt.

Her usual seat at the front of the room was free, as was the seat next to her – where Reiko had been sitting all week . . . but today, Reiko sat in the far back corner of the room, and she looked straight ahead, pointedly refusing to notice Ivy coming in.

Swallowing, Ivy forced herself to move forwards. She slumped into her seat, trying not to look as miserable as she felt. But when Olivia walked in a moment later, Ivy could see from her twin's face that it was no use. Olivia looked from Ivy to Reiko and back again.

'What's going on?' she whispered, as she took her seat by Ivy.

Ivy gave a sad shake of her head. 'I'll tell you later. For now, let's just say I have some apologising to do to Reiko on the way to our next class.'

Olivia reached out to touch her shoulder. 'I'm sure whatever you did wasn't that bad.'

'Actually . . .' Ivy winced, all too aware that Reiko would be able to hear her from across the room with her sharp vampire hearing. 'It *was* that bad,' she admitted quietly.

But I'll be a much better hostess as soon as this whole Vein of Love thing is fixed! she swore to herself.

Mr Russell, their English teacher, walked in with his usual brisk stride, and the whole class fell silent.

'Everyone, take out your pens and notebooks,' he ordered. 'We're starting today with a pop quiz.'

The rest of the class groaned, but Ivy only shrugged. *It's not like this day could get any worse.* Resigned, she leaned over to pull out a pen from her backpack . . . and froze. *Oh, no!* She'd been so distracted this morning she'd somehow not packed a single pen!

'Miss Vega?' Suddenly, Mr Russell was looming over her. 'Did I not tell everyone to take out their pens?'

129

'Ye-e-e-s.' Wincing, Ivy tried for an apologetic smile. 'But I don't actually seem to have any. I'll just have to borrow –'

'You don't have any *pens*?' Mr Russell's voice boomed through the room. 'Young lady, you may well have flashed a dazzling smile on the catwalk the other night, but in *this* school you are just an ordinary student . . . and you are expected to bring your ordinary supplies, fashion model or not!'

Snickers broke out around the room. Ivy could have melted with humiliation. 'I'm not . . . I mean, I didn't –' she stammered.

Reiko's voice interrupted her from the back of the room. 'It's my fault, sir. I borrowed Ivy's pen on the school bus, because mine was buried all the way down in my bag.' She jumped out of her seat, holding up a ballpoint pen as evidence. 'Here, Ivy. I should have remembered to give it back before class started.'

'Uh . . .' Blinking, Ivy accepted the pen, feeling

130

Mr Russell's irate gaze still resting on her. 'Thank you,' she said softly to Reiko.

'No problem.' Reiko nodded firmly to the teacher as she turned back to her own desk. 'So, everything's all right now?'

'Hmmph.' Mr Russell let out a disgruntled snort. With no student to punish, he looked as forlorn as a vampire whose Marshmallow Platelets had spilled on to the floor. 'I suppose,' he finally growled. 'But now, if everyone could please concentrate, for once . . . I can *promise* you that you will *not* enjoy this quiz!'

❤   ❤   ❤

Pop quiz or not, Ivy was in a much better mood as she left the class forty-five minutes later, with Reiko and Olivia both walking by her side.

'Thank you so much!' she said to Reiko. 'You really saved me. And I'm sorry I was so crabby before.'

'Oh, forget it. You weren't that bad!' Grinning,

131

Reiko gave her a shoulder-bump that would have knocked a human all the way across the hall. 'It was just a surprise. But I'm sorry I was so harsh, too. It's just . . .' She sighed, twirling her soccer ball on one finger again. 'I'm a little homesick, to be honest. Sport has always been my way of deflecting things that bother me.'

Olivia gave Ivy a teasing nudge. 'Oh, Ivy knows all about deflecting her emotions – don't you, Ivy?'

'Whatever.' Ivy rolled her eyes. 'But, yeah. I totally get it.'

'Anyway,' Reiko sighed, 'I keep feeling like I'm getting in the way, just by being here. So, I guess my sporty restlessness has gotten worse than usual.'

Ivy winced. 'You are definitely *not* in the way. I'm sorry if I ever made you feel like that!' She gave Reiko's arm a squeeze. 'Hey, we still have more than a week before you have to go back to

Japan. I promise to make sure you have a fantastic time. I'll even sit through a whole sports game if that's what it takes!'

Laughing, Reiko gave Ivy a hug that squeezed the soccer ball into her back. 'Thanks! By now, I know what a sacrifice that would be for you.' She stepped back, still smiling. 'But I only want to have that fantastic time *after* we've found the Vein of Love. OK?'

'Well . . .' Ivy frowned. Ahead of them, their next classroom was already coming into view. 'Being all determined *sounds* great but, honestly . . . I am *out* of ideas. I don't even know where to look next. Or *how*!'

'You will once we get to the museum after school today,' Olivia said. 'Or *I* will, anyway.' She smiled as she led the way into class. 'I have a feeling my acting training is really going to come in handy!'

'Hmm.' Ivy raised her eyebrows as she sank

down into her seat by Olivia. *I'm not sure I like the sound of that!*

♥   ♥   ♥

Ivy jumped off the school bus that afternoon and ran up Undertaker Hill as Reiko ran in the other direction, towards Sophia's parents' house.

'See you in ten minutes!' Ivy called out over her shoulder.

They were both due to meet Olivia at the museum in just twenty minutes' time, so Ivy didn't have long to pick up the replacement pashmina and drop off her books from school. The moment she stepped through her own front door, though, she came to a sudden halt.

Something's wrong.

At first, she couldn't put her finger on what was worrying her. She didn't *see* anything amiss in her front hallway . . . but the air of tension in the house was palpable. Then she heard the murmuring voices in the kitchen, sounding soft and panicked.

She walked down the hall to the kitchen and pushed the door open. 'Alex? Tessa?' She blinked. 'And . . . Dad? I thought you'd be at the museum right now.'

'Something more important came up,' Charles said. Frowning, he leaned over the breakfast bar where Prince Alex and Tessa were sitting. He handed them both steaming cups of coffee. 'Maybe these will help you feel a little better.'

'I hope so,' Tessa said sadly.

'I could definitely use some coffee right now.' Alex clutched the mug as if his life depended on it. He looked like he hadn't seen his coffin in days.

Ivy looked back and forth between the royal newlyweds. Tessa was wearing a stylish black silk blouse and skirt, and every inch of her ensemble was obviously carefully planned . . . except for the bright yellow baseball cap on her head.

'Um . . . Tessa?' Ivy frowned. 'Is that a new hat?'

There was an awkward pause.

Charles coughed. 'Ah, Ivy . . .'

Alex put a reassuring hand on his wife's shoulder. 'You don't have to talk about it if you don't want to.'

Tessa sighed. 'Oh, why clam up? Everyone will figure it out soon enough.' With a sad flourish, she pulled off the hat.

Ivy gasped.

Tessa's beautiful, silky black hair was a disaster zone. On her left side, it fell down in its usual smooth sweep, but the entire right side of her head was a shaggy, bristly, unevenly-cut mess – in places, it was less than half an inch long.

It looked exactly like the hair of the poor dolls Ivy had been given on her fifth birthday, when she was thinking she would like to be a hairdresser when she grew up.

Ouch!

'I'm so sorry,' Ivy breathed. 'But . . . what happened to you?'

Tessa looked as if she was swallowing back tears as she leaned against Alex's shoulder. 'It's a long story,' she said, 'involving chewing gum and a *really* foolish decision to self-style.' She sniffed back a sob, then gave a weary smirk. 'This holiday is certainly going to be memorable . . . but not for any of the right reasons!'

'You have had quite a run of bad luck, haven't you?' Charles sighed as he sat down at the breakfast bar beside Alex, holding his own cup of coffee. 'If I didn't know better, I'd think the Vein of Love had disappeared!'

Ivy's stomach sank. Even as the adults in the room all laughed ruefully, she fought the urge to faint – or blurt out the truth, which would be even worse.

I have to get out of here!

'I, um . . . have to go work on a big school project,' she mumbled. 'Sorry. See you guys later!'

As the adults all made sympathetic noises,

she turned and headed for the stairs, forcing herself not to run. *Look calm,* she ordered herself. *Whatever it takes!*

Even when she'd closed her bedroom door behind her, though, she couldn't stifle the panic that was filling her chest. The replacement pashmina was sitting in her desk drawer, still waiting to be taken into the museum. *I have to do it now.* Ivy took a deep breath. . . . *Before Alex and Tessa demand to see it just for their peace of mind!*

The moment they saw 'Tessa's' pashmina hanging up in the museum, they might be reassured . . . but Ivy would not be. The chain of bad luck the royal couple were experiencing right now was so outrageous, she was actually starting to wonder . . . could the curse be *real?*

It was total superstition, it was completely unlikely . . .

And yet . . .

Whatever Olivia's planning had better be brilliant,

she thought. *Because we need to find the real Vein of Love quickly – before anything even worse can happen to Alex and Tessa!*

Chapter Eight

Half an hour later, Ivy was safely inside the museum, with Olivia and Reiko by her side, and the decoy pashmina in her backpack. After a *long* discussion, Albert had finally let them in, based on the story that they were here to research a special project about vampire history.

At least that's not a total *lie*, Ivy consoled herself. Still, the vampire caretaker gave them one last, warning look as he left them in the old staff break room.

'Do not break anything!' he snapped, and closed the door behind him.

'Whew!' Reiko stretched her arms over her head. 'Are we ready?'

'I am,' Ivy replied. 'Olivia?'

But Olivia was standing completely still and silent, with her eyes closed.

Ivy watched her nervously. *Is she even still awake?*

'Olivia!' she said again, loudly. 'What in darkness are you *doing*?'

'Shh!' Olivia's eyes flashed open. 'I'm trying to find my blank slate.'

'Your *what*?' Ivy stared at her.

Olivia rolled her eyes. 'Look, we have no idea who stole the pashmina, right?'

'Right.' Ivy sighed.

'And we have no clues to go on, right?' Olivia continued.

'Right!' Reiko agreed, sounding *far* too cheery.

Ivy crossed her arms and scowled. 'So? What does that have to do with you suddenly acting like a corpse?'

'It seems to me,' Olivia said, 'that our only hope is if I can get into the head of the thief.'

'And just how is *that* supposed to happen?' Ivy massaged her own head, feeling a migraine coming on. 'You've just said we have no idea who we're looking for!'

'Ah! But if I do it right . . . the *room* will tell me.' Olivia smiled mysteriously. '*That's* why I was finding my blank slate!'

'I feel like I'm in a bad dream,' Ivy mumbled, at the same time as Reiko laughed and said: 'You Euro-American vampires really are . . . *quirky*, aren't you?'

🦇   🦇   🦇

Time to try again. Olivia turned away from Reiko to face the room and begin the process once more. But it wasn't easy to empty her mind when it was so full of bubbling worry. Panic kept trying to take her over every time she let herself wonder whether Tessa and Alex really *were* cursed – not to mention thinking about all the homework she would have to *somehow* get through tonight –

Stop! She shook herself. *This is the exact opposite of emptying my mind and finding my blank slate!*

For the next few minutes, she needed to *not* be Olivia Abbott with all of Olivia's personal worries and priorities. Instead, she needed to be a . . . *mysterious person* in the converted break room.

Taking a deep breath, she closed her eyes. *I am a blank slate. I am a blank slate. I am . . .*

When she finally opened her eyes again, she kept a silent stream of mantras in her head, blocking out all other concerns. She was a thief, looking for an opportunity. Just a thief. And . . .

Aha!

There had to be *something specific* that they wanted. No thief went to a museum thinking they might just *stumble* upon something worth taking . . .

They could have stolen something from the changing area, but they hadn't – the thief had gone for something that was *on display* in the actual museum. Had they seen it worn by Reiko and *then* sought it out?

Yes. Following the chain of intuition, Olivia hurried out the door and through the museum hallways, towards the room where the pashmina had been displayed. Some part of her brain was aware that Ivy and Reiko were following, whispering together, but she couldn't afford to let those sounds distract her.

So, I'm a thief, waiting for my opportunity . . . but why am I stealing anything in the first place?

Olivia bit her lip miserably as she felt her grip on her 'character' loosen. There had to be an answer, but what *was* it? If she could just put herself in the mind-set of someone who would steal, someone who wouldn't care what the theft might do to other people . . .

She felt outrage rise within her, as she thought of Tessa and Alex's anguished faces – but she tamped it down as she stepped into the display room, forcing herself to look around with analytical eyes, moving from one historical outfit to another as Ivy put the fake pashmina safely into place.

Maybe I'm just someone with an interest in historical artefacts? A vintage fashion buff? Or –

'Oh!' Reiko gasped.

Olivia spun around, her blank slate falling away completely. 'What happened?'

'Look at this!' Reiko was leaning over behind a display cabinet on the far side of the room, picking something off the floor. 'It's a receipt from One Planet – that wonderful health food store you two took me to last Sunday! And the date on the receipt is from Wednesday.'

'The day of the fashion show.' Ivy narrowed her eyes. 'The museum was not open to the public on Wednesday, and it's been closed ever since then . . .'

'Ohhh . . .' Olivia turned in a circle, scoping out the whole room. 'Yes!' she breathed. 'I can *see* it now. The receipt must have fallen out of the thief's pocket as they crouched down to hide behind that display cabinet when you and Penny came into the room with the pashmina . . .'

'. . . or maybe,' Ivy finished grimly, 'it fell out when they scrambled from behind the display cabinet, taking their chance when the lights went off.'

'Can I see the receipt?' Olivia asked Reiko.

'Sure.' Reiko passed it over.

'Hmm.' Olivia tapped the top of the receipt with one pale-pink fingernail. 'This doesn't just have a date — it also has a time. The thief was at One Planet just before coming to the museum for the opening of Café Creative.' Smiling triumphantly, she met her sister's gaze. 'Why

146

don't we head over there now and see if any clerk remembers this particular order?'

🦇   🦇   🦇

Well, it felt *like a good plan,* Olivia thought glumly, twenty minutes later. *Maybe if we hadn't come with Reiko, it might even have worked!*

Unfortunately, taking Reiko to her favourite health food store had been too much for the exchange student's willpower. One Planet had been nearly empty when they'd first arrived – which was perfect for their investigation – but the moment Olivia and Ivy had reached the counter and opened their mouths to start asking questions, Reiko had completely lost control.

'Oh, I can't wait. I *need* one of your Vitali-Teas right now! They're just so good, I've been thinking about my last one ever since Sunday.'

'Aren't they fabulous?' The server, a blonde woman in her mid-twenties whose nametag read "Norah", nodded vigorously, leaning across the counter. 'I don't even feel awake before my shots of gotu kola any more! What I *really* love about it is . . .'

Olivia traded a horrified look with Ivy as the two health food fans launched into an endless discussion about gotu kola versus caffeine. Over the next five minutes, they moved on to raves about tofu, sprouts, wheatgrass, and then some foods Olivia had never even heard of before! It was only when the bell over the door rang, signalling a whole crowd of new arrivals, that Norah finally jumped back from the counter.

'Oops! I'd better start making your Vitali-Tea. Looks like I'm about to be swamped!'

Olivia swallowed a groan as she looked at the crowd of over ten people already forming a line behind them. From the looks on their faces, they were impatient for their gotu kola, too . . . and if she and Ivy held up the server by asking investigative questions, the impatient customers

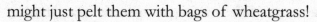

might just pelt them with bags of wheatgrass!

Olivia shook her head as she turned back to the server, who was facing away from them. Ironically, Norah wore a rather fabulous pashmina herself, although hers was sunflower-yellow.

'We'll need to plan this *very* carefully,' Olivia mumbled to Ivy out of the corner of her mouth. 'Can you do a good "indecisive"?'

'Absolutely not,' Ivy said. 'I'm not the actress in this family, remember? How about *you* play the indecisive one, while I ask the hard questions?'

'OK.' Olivia let out her breath. 'You know, I'm actually more comfortable with that idea!'

Norah turned back, beaming and holding out a large cup of Vitali-Tea.

'Ohh!' Reiko snatched it out of her hands. 'I'm so excited!'

'And what would you two like?' Norah asked, turning expectantly to Ivy and Olivia. Behind

149

them, the line rustled as people prepared to shuffle forward.

'Umm . . .' Olivia tried to look anguished as she leaned over the glass display case set inside the counter. 'I just can*not* decide. I've been looking at those vegan truffles, and they look soooo amazing – but then those almond butter chews look so good, too, I think . . . I think . . . oh!' She put her hands in her hair, tugging as if she could force herself to think. 'I just need one more moment . . .'

She leaned over until she was nearly pressing her nose against the glass, ignoring the huffs and groans of the crowd waiting behind her. She heard the rustle of paper as Ivy handed over the receipt to Norah.

'While she's making up her mind, can I ask: does this receipt ring any bells for you?'

'Excuse me?' Norah sounded startled. 'I'm not sure I –'

150

'We're trying to figure out who dropped it,' Ivy explained. 'They left behind something really important, too, along with the receipt, and we want to get it back to them. But we need to figure out who we're looking for . . .'

'Well, in that case . . .' Norah paused. 'Let me think.'

Olivia slid a glance up out of the corner of her eyes to see Norah frowning over the receipt.

'Oh, *wait*!' Suddenly, the server flashed a bright smile. 'There's only *one* regular customer of ours who *always* orders oatmeal with avocado, plus an extra-large serving of Vitali-Tea.'

She passed the receipt back to Ivy and nodded firmly. 'I know exactly who you're looking for.'

They all leaned forwards.

'You do?' asked Olivia, abandoning any pretence of ordering.

A tall man pushed up next to her at the counter. 'One extra-large Vitali-Tea to go, please.'

151

Norah picked up a cup and then turned back to the girls. 'Yes, that's Maxie Richards,' she said as she flipped on the Vitali-Tea machine. 'Great kid.' The machine whirred into life, hissing and bubbling loudly. Norah was still saying something and Olivia strained her ears to hear, '. . . Wednesdays after art class . . . over from Lincoln Vale . . .'

'What does she look like?' Ivy asked, over the noise.

'What?' Norah called.

'Looks!' Ivy pointed to her hair and face.

'Oh! Well . . . about fifteen, I'd say . . . eyes and shoulder-length brown hair.'

Olivia could barely hear a thing. 'I'm sorry, what −' She could not finish her question, because more customers were pushing forward.

Norah shook her head. 'Sorry, kids!'

Realising that this was all they were going to get, they turned away from the counter.

As they marched out of One Planet, Olivia saw Ivy fix an imaginary person with a death-squint. 'OK, Maxie Richards with brown hair from Lincoln Vale . . . The Daring Detective Duo are going to find you!'

Reiko made a show of clearing her throat, and Ivy looked sheepish.

'I mean, the Daring Detective *Trio*.'

Chapter Nine

The next morning, Olivia stepped through the big glass doors of the Lincoln Vale and felt a sense of déja-vu. The last time she and Ivy had come here with a friend, they'd been tracking another suspicious girl through the mall, just as they were today. This time, though, they were on the trail of a thief; and instead of Sophia coming with them, they had Reiko, whose hair today was a rather "Altegular" chaos of pink and black streaks. Her trademark tennis racquet stuck up out of her backpack as she looked around with cheerful curiosity.

I bet she wasn't expecting this to be a part of her

exchange programme! Olivia thought. But she couldn't spare any time to worry about that. She was too busy scanning left and right, down the long, wide corridors of the upscale mall. They had figured that most Lincoln Vale teens could be found in the mall at the weekends and they hadn't been wrong – but the place was so crowded, they felt no closer to finding Maxie Richards.

Is Maxie short for Maxine, I wonder?

'OK, we can't just walk up and down all day.' Ivy came to a halt, frowning. 'We need a plan. I think we're most likely to have success if we scope out the clothing stores.'

Olivia nodded. 'Well, we do know Maxie has a thing for clothing . . .'

'And since this whole incident has been a fashion frightmare,' Ivy added, 'it makes sense that our thief girl would be the type to frequent a niche boutique or two. How about Blue Skye's?'

Olivia shuddered. 'I don't know . . . The last

time we went, Blue Skye tried to get mall security to arrest us!'

'Whoa!' Reiko bounced on the tips of her tennis shoes. 'Exactly what kind of trouble did you two get up to? And what kind of store *is* it, anyway?'

'Oh, just New Age clothes.' Ivy shrugged. 'Lots of incense. You know, typical.'

'But the owner is *not* typical at all!' Olivia grimaced. 'I mean, she's very laid back about *most* things . . . but when it comes to customers "just browsing", she morphs from "Blue Skye" into "Red Skye"!' She shook her head vigorously, backing away from Ivy. 'Seriously, we had to run for our lives last time we visited.'

'I'm not thrilled to go back there, either,' Ivy agreed. 'But just think about it: if Maxie has such a liking for pashminas, doesn't it make sense that she would shop at Blue Skye's?'

'Ugh.' Olivia groaned, dropping her head in

defeat. 'I *hate* it when you make sense . . . about something I *really* don't want to do!'

But her steps only dragged a little bit as she followed her twin towards Blue Skye's shop. Today, the display window was draped with gauzy fabrics, and a curtain of colourful beads hung in the doorway. Taking a deep breath, Olivia ducked through the curtain, tiny beads jangling and bumping against her skin on all sides.

She winced at the loud tinkling of the wind chimes that were hung all over the place. Olivia found it almost impossible to move without making them jingle. She tripped and fell straight into a huge one. Ivy and Reiko both clasped their hands to their ears and moaned. It was too much for their super vamp hearing to take!

Mouthing 'Sorry!', Olivia straightened up, forced herself to breathe deeply and took a good look around the shop.

There was only one other customer inside

– a long-haired boy about their age who was browsing through a colourful collection of scarves, pashminas, saris and sarongs on the opposite wall. He fingered one purple-and-yellow cotton sarong with a thoughtful look on his face. Usually, in a shop like this, Olivia would only have expected to see boys waiting impatiently for their girlfriends, or simply looking lost, but this boy actually seemed to know what he was doing.

Too bad. Olivia sighed and turned away. If he'd actually needed help, he *might* have distracted the attention of Blue Skye. Speaking of whom . . .

'Welcome, friends!' Blue Skye's voice boomed out just behind Olivia, making her jump. 'Have we met before?'

'Um . . .?' Olivia flashed a desperate glance at her sister.

Ivy removed one hand from her ear and pointed wordlessly behind Olivia. Slowly, reluctantly, Olivia turned to face the shop owner.

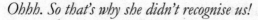

Ohhh. So that's why she didn't recognise us!

Blue Skye was an unmistakable figure, clothed in gauzy, rippling layers of bright blue, green, and yellow silk from the top of her head to her gold-painted toenails. But what Olivia noticed most of all was the thin, black silk scarf wrapped around her eyes.

'I'm so sorry!' Olivia said. 'Did we wake you up from a nap?' She wouldn't have expected most shop owners to go to sleep in the middle of the daytime, in their own shops, but Blue Skye was not 'most shop owners'.

'You're asking about my little blindfold, aren't you?' Blue Skye chuckled indulgently as she patted the silk over her eyes. 'No, I have simply reached a higher level of experience. That thing which we call "sight"? That only gets in the way of *really seeing* the world around us!' Her voice rolled out with all the intensity of a politician campaigning for votes. 'When we open our eyes, we become blind to the truth *beyond* our vision!'

Reiko looked fascinated. 'But . . . don't you walk into things – like, all the time?'

'Pfft.' Blue Skye waved the question away with one sweep of her arm. 'My goal is to improve my *true* vision. What does it matter if I suffer a few boring bumps and bruises along the way? Honestly, the physical is *so* overrated.'

Ivy cleared her throat. 'Uh . . . it might not be *that* overrated . . .'

'What do you mean?' Blue Skye swung around, turning to face Ivy's direction. 'Do you dare dispute my vision, visitor?'

'Well . . .' Ivy coughed. 'It's just, I can see quite a few empty hangers and racks around the store.' She shrugged. 'I think someone may have taken advantage of your experiment, Blue Skye. You've been robbed!'

Something crashed at the other side of the shop. Olivia spun around to see the boy at the other side of the store looking as shocked as if Ivy had poked him with a stick. The clothing rack behind him had been knocked backwards – he must have jumped when he'd heard her words. He pointedly replaced the sarong he'd been holding and backed away with his empty hands held high.

Oops! Olivia gave an apologetic smile – clearly, he'd thought Ivy was accusing him of the clothing thefts! He only ducked his head in response to her smile, though, turning around so fast he nearly tripped over his own feet. He then speed-walked the rest of the way out of the shop, sending the curtain of beads jangling with his exit.

'Oh, nonsense.' Blue Skye let out such a massive snort, the gauzy silk hood around her head ruffled in its breeze. 'That's the problem with our culture nowadays – this inhibiting belief that everything has to *cost* something.'

'Er . . .?' Ivy looked at the price tags on the clothes hanging near her. 'We are in a store –'

'Ah, but money cannot buy you time, can it? Or peace, or love?' Blue Skye shook her head, her tone weary. 'Trust me, young one: the sooner we *all* realise that, the happier we will be.'

This is getting us nowhere! Olivia's breath whistled out through her gritted teeth in a noise that was half-growl and half-sigh. A *grigh*!

At the sound, Blue Skye swung around to face Olivia. With her blindfolded eyes, the movement looked strangely eerie, especially when she sniffed loudly, as if following a scent. 'I can sense – oh yes – I have seekers in my shop today. Seekers who need my help!'

'Well . . .' Olivia blinked, slightly taken aback. 'I guess you could say that.'

'Of course. My inner vision grows strong.' Smiling serenely, Blue Skye placed both be-ringed hands on her chest. 'I will provide all the help

162

that I possibly can. Come!' She swept around and headed purposefully for the counter, neatly side-stepping all the clothes-racks in her path.

Olivia watched with reluctant awe as Blue Skye cut a clear path through the cluttered shop, bypassing clothing racks, jewellery displays and glass cabinets, despite her blindfold. *Maybe she is developing inner vision after all!*

Ivy didn't stop to watch. Instead, she hurried after Blue Skye, frowning intently. 'Do you know all your regular customers?'

'Ohhh . . .' Blue Skye shrugged, sending her gauzy layers shifting all around her like an ocean in a storm. 'Can any person truly *know* another person, in their heart of hearts?'

Olivia could feel another grigh building up inside her. She had to slam her mouth shut to keep it in . . .

For once, Ivy seemed to be keeping her cool. 'I take your point,' she said calmly, 'but we're looking for someone – someone who may need our help – and we're running out of ideas for how to find them.'

Otherwise, we certainly wouldn't have come here! Olivia added silently. But she kept her mouth shut as she watched Blue Skye's face smooth out in pleasure.

'You have come to the right place, seekers,' the shop owner announced. She set the palms of her hands together and cocked her hooded and blindfolded head to one side, waiting with unnerving poise. 'Tell me.'

'OK.' Ivy leaned across the counter. 'We have reason to believe that Maxie might shop here.'

'Maxie?' Blue Skye's lips curved into a smile. 'Are you talking about Maxie Richards, by any chance?'

'Yes!' Olivia couldn't help the squeak of delight that escaped her lips.

Ivy leaned towards Blue Skye. 'Can you give

us an idea of who it is we're looking for? All we know so far is that Maxie has shoulder-length brown hair.'

'I have no idea what Maxie *looks* like,' Blue Skye answered.

'What?' Olivia's mouth dropped open.

Ivy shook her head. 'You just said you know Maxie Richards. So how can you *not* know what Maxie looks like?'

'Perfectly easily,' Blue Skye said. 'You see, Maxie has only started shopping here in the last couple of weeks or so, and in that time . . .' She let out a low, purring hum of satisfaction and pointed to her blindfold. 'I have not laid eyes on a single person. And, I have to say, if all you care about is frivolous, shallow physical detail, I don't know how much help I can be.'

Olivia clapped her hands to her head. *You can say that again!* She had always believed in compassion and tolerance – but, while it was great that Blue Skye was trying to mellow out and believe in the goodness underneath other people's surfaces, Olivia wondered how sensible such an approach was when it led to her getting robbed . . . *and* being no help at all in the twins' Pashmina Panic?

Sighing, Ivy stepped back from the counter. 'Thanks anyway,' she said to Blue Skye. 'We appreciate the help.'

'Of course.' Blue Skye lowered her chin in a regal nod. 'You may always come back to this shop, seekers, when you desire a brush with true inner vision . . . or, of course, when what you desire is a really lovely piece of clothing, designed especially for the inner you.'

'Thank you,' Olivia mumbled. She knew she didn't sound enthusiastic, but right now, it was the very best that she could do, with yet another grigh building inside her.

'What are we going to do?' she whispered to

166

Ivy as they started out of the store.

Ivy didn't bother to whisper back. 'I don't know,' she said glumly. 'Short of asking every customer in the mall, I have no idea how we're going to find her now.'

'Oh, you won't.' Blue Skye's voice boomed through the store. 'Trust me, seekers. You won't find her.'

'Huh?' Ivy's voice finally took on an edge as she swung back towards the blindfolded shop-keeper. '*Why* won't we find her? Oh, let me guess. Because we're not –' She crooked her fingers into air-quotes that Blue Skye had no chance of seeing –'"looking in the right space"? Or because our "open eyes are really locked shut"?'

Uh-oh. Olivia braced herself. *I think the Skye is about to turn Red!*

But Blue Skye's lips curled an extra half-inch higher in their smile as she leaned forward, her hood dropping lower over her forehead. 'No, my dears,' she murmured gently. 'Because there is no "her" to find. Didn't you realise? Maxie Richards is a boy!'

Olivia clutched at Ivy's arm. They stared at each other in sudden, wild surprise.

Why didn't it ever even occur to me that 'Maxie' could be a boy? Olivia wondered. *But if he is . . .*

'Actually . . .' Blue Skye tilted her head back to sniff the air. 'I think I recognise his scent – oh, yes. Patchouli oil and lavender. Unmistakable.' She lowered her chin to her chest. 'Yes, he was here not long ago. But, how odd. He usually says hello.'

'I know why he didn't this time,' Ivy said grimly.

'Of course,' Olivia breathed. The boy who'd been there when they'd first arrived, the one who'd browsed so purposefully through the sarongs, who looked like he knew exactly what he was doing . . . *That* was Maxie!

168

And he'd left like a startled cat the moment Ivy had mentioned the subject of *thefts*.

'He can't have got too far away,' said Reiko. She was already bouncing on her toes, warming up for action. 'He might still be in the mall!'

'Let's go!' Ivy lunged for the exit.

🦇   🦇   🦇

I can say one thing about trips to Blue Skye's shop, Ivy thought as she ducked through the curtain of beads. *They're always memorable!*

Ivy had to force herself to take deep, calming breaths as she thought through her strategy. If she wanted to, she could race through the whole mall in a blur, but that would risk exposing the vampire secret – a gamble she would never take. *If only vamps could make themselves invisible!*

Instead, she led Olivia and Reiko to the escalator that led up to the mezzanine level. 'Come on. What we need is a raised platform to stand on, so we can get the best view of the whole mall.'

'Makes sense.' Olivia nodded firmly as the escalator lifted them up, while Reiko scanned the scene around them with wide-eyed interest.

Ivy counted down seconds until they reached the top. 'Finally!' She lunged forwards to look over the glass banister at the shifting crowds beneath them. All she needed now was . . .

Wait a minute. She frowned. 'Can either of you two remember, clearly, what the guy in Blue Skye's store looked like?' As much as Ivy tried, all she could envision was his black shirt – something that half the boys *and* girls downstairs were wearing. 'I was so sure Maxie was a girl, I didn't even take a second look at him when he was in the shop.'

'Me neither,' Reiko said.

'Um . . .' Making a rueful face, Olivia shrugged. 'I think . . . he might have been wearing blue jeans? Or black?'

'Great.' Ivy slumped against the banister. 'That *really* narrows it down.'

'Sorry.' Olivia winced.

'Don't be.' Ivy sighed. 'It's not your fault. But
. . . aagh! Our best lead just slipped through our
fingers. He was *right in front* of us – and we still
can't find him!' She dropped her head on to her
forearms. 'Some investigator I am!'

'Hey.' Olivia patted her shoulder. 'Don't you
think you're forgetting something?'

'Like what?' Ivy mumbled. 'My brain? My
observational skills? My –?'

'No,' Olivia said. 'Your *nose*! Don't you
remember what Blue Skye said? Maxie wears a
scent of patchouli oil and lavender. That can't
be a common combo on most of the guys
shopping here today, can it? And with you and
Reiko both sharing that heightened sense of
smell . . .' Her smile sounded in her voice. 'All is
not definitely lost!'

'Of course.' Ivy shook her head with a mixture
of relief and fury. *How could I not have thought of*

that? I can be such a useless vamp sometimes.

She looked to Reiko, who was tilting back her head to scent the air. Then the exchange student gave a worried grimace. 'Actually,' she said, 'my nose isn't working quite right in America. Everything smells the same to me here!'

Ivy turned to face the crowds below. It looked like it was all on her now. 'Come on,' she muttered to herself. 'Focus!'

But every time she tried to follow the scents in the air, she found herself distracted by the movements of the people beneath her. 'Why can't I stop *looking*?'

'I have an idea.' Reiko pulled her backpack off her shoulder and rummaged inside.

Ivy frowned. 'You want to play a game *now*?'

'Better.' Reiko pulled out a sweatband. 'Ta-da!'

'Um . . .' Ivy's eyes widened. 'I really don't think –'

But Reiko was already advancing purposefully.

'I promise it's totally clean,' she said, as she yanked it down over Ivy's eyes. 'How's that?'

'How *is* it?' Ivy almost laughed. 'I'm *blind*, that's how it is. Why in darkness – *oh* . . . Wait . . .' Her nose gave an involuntary twitch. 'I'm getting something!'

'I knew it,' Reiko said. 'I got the idea from Blue Skye!'

Normally, Ivy might have rolled her eyes, but this time, she didn't even say a snarky word. Because right there, floating in the middle of the riot of scents that filled the crowded mall, was . . .

Patchouli oil and lavender. 'This way!'

She started forwards, but arms pulled her back.

'Wait!' Olivia was saying. 'You were about to walk right into everyone getting off the escalator! Should I take this thing off you?'

'No!' Ivy slapped one protective hand against the sweatband, holding it tight. 'I need it to keep my focus. Just get me on to the "down" escalator, back to the ground floor – and don't let me knock into anything!'

Olivia and Reiko guided her through the crowd of people until Ivy felt her hand touch the rubber guide rail of the escalator. As the moving stairs carried her down towards the source of that "Maxie" scent, whispers rose – and her vampire hearing, strengthened by her blindness, caught them all.

'Whoa! Look at that pale girl with the blindfold!'

'What is she doing?'

'Maybe it's a dare.'

'Maybe she's got some kind of sickness.'

'Or, maybe . . . she's just *really* weird.'

Reiko must have heard the whispers too. 'It's a treasure hunt!' she called out from behind Ivy. 'She's sniffing out prizes!'

'Cool!' The people in front of them on the escalator started peppering Reiko and Olivia with

174

questions about the treasure hunt and some of them started sniffing the air curiously.

Ivy ignored them all, her attention focused on that single thread of scent. The moment her feet hit solid ground, she started to her right.

'Uh-uh!' Olivia tugged her left. 'This way.'

'*No!*' Gritting her teeth, Ivy pulled to her right with all her strength.

It should have been no contest – and it would not have been, if Olivia was the only person pulling Ivy. But she was teamed up with a vampire and, together, the two girls yanked her hard, and Ivy staggered to her left, barely staying upright.

'What are you *doing*?' she hissed. 'Maxie is *this* way!'

'Well, so is a handbag stand,' Olivia said sharply, 'and you were about to walk straight into it!'

'Oh.' Ivy stopped resisting. 'Thanks. But we need to go in the other direction!'

'No worries.' Reiko sounded as cheerful as ever. 'Olivia and I can guide you around the stand.'

With both of their hands on her arms, Ivy shuffled in a half-circle, hanging on to Maxie's scent with all her focus. The shifting crowd around her was full of other smells, from perfume to sweat, leather and fresh-baked cookies, but with every step, Maxie's scent grew stronger. In fact, it was *so* strong and steady, Ivy was almost certain that the boy had stayed in one place for at least the last few minutes.

Excellent. For once, he might actually be easy to find!

'This way,' she whispered, tugging the others with her. 'This way, this way . . . stop!'

Ivy reached up and yanked her blindfold off.

Bright lights glowed above her, revealing rows and rows of comic books.

They were standing inside Tall Tony's Comic Book Emporium . . .

And standing across the room from them, browsing one of the colourful displays, was Maxie Richards.

Chapter Ten

I vy started forwards.

Before she could take a second step, a skinny, pink-haired man in a bright yellow anime T-shirt popped out from behind the front counter.

'Hey, dudes! I'm Tall Tony. Can I help you find anything?'

'Um . . .' Ivy frowned, distracted by the big-eyed girl on his T-shirt. *He's a little too old to pull that off.* 'We're just browsing, actu–' She cringed as she caught herself too late.

Oh, no. I said the dreaded B-word!

Ivy gave herself a mental slap. Today's

encounter with the new-and-improved Blue Skye had lulled her into thinking browsing might actually be OK, but what if Tall Tony was of the Blue Skye 1.0 style of store owner? 'Um . . .' Quickly, Ivy gathered her wits. 'When I said "browsing",' she began, 'what I really meant was . . . was . . .'

'Hey, it's all cool, dude.' Tony gave her a sleepy smile. 'Browsing is how we make our greatest discoveries.' Still smiling, he ambled back to his seat behind the counter and picked up a graphic novel. A moment later, he was laughing quietly to himself as he read, apparently oblivious to the world around him.

'Wow,' Olivia breathed into Ivy's ear. 'If Tony's single, maybe we should see if we can match him with the new-and-improved Blue Skye. They seem like a perfect match!'

'Hmm . . .' Ivy tilted her head, seriously considering the question. 'I'm not so sure about that one. Do you think they'd ever actually *make* it to a date?'

'Good point.' Olivia grinned mischievously. 'Scheduling an exact date and time would be much too rigid for Blue Skye.'

'Yup. They'd have to just happen to both end up in the same place at the same time by some kind of "cosmic accident"!'

Olivia burst into laughter, and Ivy couldn't help but join in. After all the stress and exhaustion of the last week, the whole thing was too ridiculous to even think about with a straight face. But if a cosmically-ordered date ever did work out for the two store owners . . . what would they name their joint store? *Blue Tony? Tall Skye?* Or . . .

'Ahem!' Reiko cleared her throat, staring at them as if they'd both gone crazy. 'Aren't we here for a reason?' She tipped her head meaningfully in the direction of the boy across the room, who was still engrossed in his comic book.

There's no mistaking where he shops! Ivy thought. If his long, pale blue shirt made of knobbly hemp had *not* come from Blue Skye's store it had to have come straight from a tropical island, just like the billowing cotton trousers he wore underneath it. His brown hair was long enough to curl at the bottom of his neck, and she thought that even Olivia would be able to smell the patchouli oil on his skin from the other side of Tall Tony's.

'Oops.' Still grinning, Olivia stepped back. 'Reiko's right. It's time for the Daring Detective Duo – well, *Trio* – to take action!'

Ivy nodded, starting across the room with quiet, stealthy steps – like a tiger stalking her prey. Maxie's back was still turned to them, even as he set down his comic book and moved over to the collectibles' stand. From the way he was bent, he seemed to be studying the limited edition superhero figurines, along with spaceships in the shape of . . . bats.

Ivy winced. *Well, that's appropriate, anyway,* she thought ruefully . . . but then she stopped.

Reiko and Olivia almost walked straight into her.

'What's wrong?' Reiko hissed.

Ivy shook her head. 'I was so determined to catch up with him, I didn't even think about a plan! How are we going to strike up a conversation with a boy like this?'

'Hmm.' Olivia frowned. 'I don't know anything about comics . . . or figurines!'

'*Exactly,*' Ivy said. 'None of us does! And how exactly are we supposed to broach the whole topic of the pashmina theft? We can't just walk up and say, *We know you stole it!*'

'No-o-o,' Olivia said doubtfully. 'But we have to do *something*. Maybe . . .'

Reiko heaved a loud sigh and adjusted her backpack. 'Leave this to me.'

Ivy leaped back just in time to avoid getting

hit on the head by the handle of Reiko's tennis racquet as the exchange student strode confidently across the room. She nudged Maxie in the arm. 'Hey! What do you think of that X-5000 model? I don't like it as much as last month's version!'

Ivy's mouth dropped open. She turned to stare at Olivia, and found her twin looking just as flabbergasted as Ivy felt.

Is this really happening?

Across the room, Maxie and Reiko were quickly engaged in a heated debate.

As Ivy listened in shock, Reiko's voice rose. '. . . but the extra side-fins make *all* the difference! Just think: how would they have coped in Issue 512 if it hadn't been for those?'

'It's like she's speaking a different language,' Ivy hissed to her twin. 'I will *never* understand this girl!'

Olivia's shoulders rose in a helpless shrug. 'I

guess . . . she's sporty *and* a comic book fan. So? People can have multiple interests.'

'Yeah, but . . .' Ivy let out a frustrated breath. 'Look, it's not that I think a person can't be into two different things. I would *never* think that made anyone fake or un-cool, or anything like that. It's just . . . where does Reiko find the *time* to have all these interests? I barely even manage to watch *Shadowtown* these days!'

Olivia gave her a rueful smile. 'Maybe Reiko doesn't spend all her time solving mysteries!'

'Hmmph.' Ivy rolled her eyes at her twin. Trying to be discreet, she drifted closer to the collectibles' stand, aware of Olivia following close behind. 'Shh,' she whispered.

She shouldn't have worried. From the passion in the two fans' voices, they wouldn't have noticed if a herd of elephants had stampeded past them.

'You've read that one too?' Maxie's voice shot

up with delight. 'I *love* the art in that issue!'

'It's really great, isn't it?' Reiko nodded so hard, her pink-and-black ponytail bobbed wildly behind her. 'I just wish I could draw that well myself!'

'I know what you mean . . .' Maxie's head ducked. He sounded shy as he mumbled. 'Art is my big passion. I'd love to work in comics one day. It would be amazing – I just hope I'm good enough.'

'That is so cool!' Reiko paused, glancing past Maxie at Ivy and Olivia. 'So . . .' She cleared her throat. 'I'm only here for another week, but even *I* know about Café Creative. That was a *definite* highlight of my trip. If you're an artist, you must have been at the opening night, too. What did you think of it?'

Go, Reiko! Ivy cheered silently as Maxie's head jerked up. Anticipation filled her as she saw the sudden panic on his face. *Come on,* she urged him silently, *just admit you were at the scene of the crime!*

'Well . . . yeah . . . I mean, I heard it was pretty cool.' He shifted nervously from one foot to another, looking like he might turn and run at any moment.

'You *heard* it was cool?' Ivy sidled up behind him. He jumped at the sudden new voice. 'Are you saying that you didn't go? I thought practically *everyone* in Franklin Grove and Lincoln Vale stopped by the opening of the café that night. The place was *packed*.'

'It really was.' Olivia stepped up on his other side, neatly boxing him in.

Maxie's gaze darted from one girl to the next. 'Um . . .'

Ivy studied him closely. *This is no hardened thief.*

Maybe Maxie *had* taken the pashmina – but now that she'd heard him talking so passionately about art with Reiko, Ivy was getting the feeling there was a more complicated explanation for what had happened. And after all her sleepless nights, she was ready to hear it *now*.

She forced her expression to harden as she put forward her best bluff. 'I could have sworn I saw you there, at the launch . . .'

'Oh, um, I couldn't get a ticket.' Maxie's shoulders hunched as his gaze dropped. 'They sold out so fast.'

'Yeah?' Ivy arched one eyebrow menacingly. 'I'm *sure* I saw you around the place, though.'

Olivia's eyes narrowed. 'Maybe you were at the museum *before* the launch started?'

Wow, Ivy thought. *Olivia's really putting her acting skills to use! I've never seen her look so stern.*

'Um . . .' Now Maxie's skin looked chalk-white. He moistened his lips nervously.

A whirring noise sounded overhead, and cold air suddenly blasted down at them from the overhead air conditioner. *Perfect*, Ivy thought.

She rubbed her hands up and down her

arms. 'Oof, that's cold. If only I had something I could use to get *warm*.'

'Something you could drape over your shoulders, maybe?' Olivia said pointedly.

Reiko crossed her arms. 'Like a pashmina, you mean?'

'Oh, no . . .' Maxie let out a weary sigh as his shoulders slumped. 'How could you have *possibly* found out?'

The look of defeat on his face was so pitiful, Ivy had to bite back the triumphant grin that wanted to break out on her face. 'Sorry,' she said lightly. 'But we're good at this kind of thing.'

She looked over his shoulders at Olivia and Reiko, and both of them grinned back at her.

The Daring Detective Trio has solved the mystery!

Ten minutes later, all four of them were gathered around a table in the mall food court. Not only had they wanted a more private place to talk, but Maxie had looked ready to faint with shock, so Olivia had declared food an urgent medical emergency.

For him anyway, Ivy thought, and sighed. Maxie and Olivia were both nibbling at pita pockets with hummus as they sat across the table from her, but she and Reiko had been left empty-handed. 'Veggie Val's' was hardly a vampire-friendly foodstand.

She traded a rueful look with Reiko as Maxie finished his pita and let out a sigh of obvious satisfaction. Hunger growled in her own stomach, but she tried to ignore it.

'OK,' she said. 'Now that you've eaten, it's time to finally tell us the truth.'

Maxie took a deep breath and then sighed: 'It's all Penny Taylor's fault.'

Olivia made a choking noise and Ivy stared at him. 'What?'

Maxie blushed and stared at the table. 'Well,

not really,' he said. 'It's my fault but I just . . . I just wanted her to notice me.'

'You stole a pashmina because you wanted Penny to *notice* you?' Ivy said slowly.

Olivia frowned. 'Were you going to wear it?'

Reiko snorted and then burst out laughing. Even Maxie gave a small smile. 'No, I wasn't.' He grimaced. 'I guess I'd better tell you the whole story . . . no matter how embarrassing it is.'

Ivy couldn't quite bring herself to give him one of her patented death-squints, but she folded her arms as firmly as she could. 'I think that would be a good idea.'

'OK.' Maxie seemed to steel himself. 'Penny Taylor used to go to Lincoln Vale Middle School with me. We were friends, but I've always . . . liked her a lot.'

'Penny *is* great,' said Olivia warmly. She gave Maxie an encouraging smile and Ivy shot her a look. *This is an interrogation, not a dating show!*

'I really want Penny to notice me,' Maxie continued, 'but we don't see each other much any more. She goes to Franklin Grove High now and she's busy with her art and fashion design.'

'We heard that you are into art as well,' said Olivia.

Ivy rolled her eyes. Why could her twin not *focus* on this?

Maxie was nodding. 'That's what Penny and I have in common. So I decided to come to the opening of Café Creative and talk to her. After the show, I followed you and Penny to the display room. I saw you with the pashmina and I thought it would be the perfect talking point. But then I panicked and I hid. I was just trying to work up the courage to come out from behind the display case and ask her about the pashmina and its designs, but she started to leave before I worked up the nerve.'

He ran a hand through his long hair, nervously

tapping his knuckles on the table as he tried to continue his story.

'I didn't want to lose my chance. So I thought, maybe if I went over and made a big show of admiring the pashmina, she might hear me and turn around, and then . . .' He drifted off, looking hopeless.

'It *might* have worked,' Reiko said thoughtfully. 'If you'd said something really cool afterwards.'

'I suck at "cool" conversation,' Maxie said sadly. 'I was so desperate, though, I would have tried anything. But before I could say a word, the lights went out.'

'I remember.' Ivy's eyes narrowed. 'So what happened then?'

Maxie shrugged. 'It was so dark, I was . . . as blind as Blue Skye. I was just fumbling around, trying to find my way out, when I felt myself knock the pashmina off its stand. I *freaked out*. I mean, it's probably priceless – what if I'd

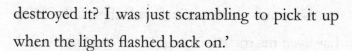

destroyed it? I was just scrambling to pick it up when the lights flashed back on.'

'And then?' Ivy prompted.

He looked miserable. 'I panicked. I was about to be caught in a place I shouldn't have been – and I still didn't even know yet if I'd damaged the pashmina! I didn't even think. I just ran.' He sighed, setting his hands flat on the table. 'It wasn't until I was outside that I even realised I was actually still carrying it. I should have dropped it back in the museum, but by the time I noticed . . . it was too late. So I just kept running.'

'Oh, Maxie.' Olivia shook her head. 'If only you'd come back –'

'I know,' Maxie said, sighing heavily. 'But my fear got the best of me. I just tore down the fire escape. I knew that if anyone caught me, they'd never believe my story, so . . .'

'Wrong,' Ivy said firmly. '*I* believe your story, and none of us are planning to tell on you.'

193

'Absolutely not,' Reiko said cheerfully. 'This has been the most exciting part of my trip so far!'

'We don't want to get anyone in trouble,' Olivia said. 'We just need to get the pashmina back to the museum.'

'And *fast*,' Ivy added. *Before Alex and Tessa can get dive-bombed by any more angry birds!* Superstition or not, she wouldn't feel like their royal friends were safe until the real pashmina was resting securely in the museum again.

'But how?' Maxie looked at her with big, pleading eyes. 'I've been trying to think of a way to sneak it back into the museum, but the building's been locked up every day since the fashion show! How am I supposed to put it back now?'

'Hmm.' Drumming her black-nailed fingers on the table, Ivy looked away for a moment. The museum had re-opened that morning, but any crowds might make their job even harder. How were they going to make sure that the display room was empty when they snuck the pashmina back inside?

Her gaze fell on Olivia, who was frowning with obvious concentration. 'What is it?' Ivy asked. 'Do you have any good ideas?'

Olivia gave a start. 'What? Oh, I wasn't even thinking about that part.' She turned to Maxie, beaming. 'I was thinking how we can get you set up with Penny.'

Maxie's face flushed bright pink. 'Oh no, it's . . . You really don't need . . . She doesn't like me.' He looked away and mumbled. 'I have no chance.'

Ivy nudged her sister's foot under the table. 'Um, Olivia? Don't we have something more important to deal with right now?' *Like a vampire curse!*

'Pfft!' Olivia snorted, waving off the interruption. 'What could be more important than love . . .? Aha!' She jumped in her seat, pointing a triumphant finger at Maxie. 'You blushed even more when I said that word! Don't deny it, Maxie. You're in love, aren't you?'

Maxie's whole face was a bright, giveaway red, all the way down to the bottom of his neck. 'It's just hopeless,' he mumbled.

'Nothing is hopeless,' said Olivia firmly. 'Not with me in charge, anyway.'

For a moment, Maxie stared at her in shock. Then he swallowed visibly. 'You mean it? You would actually help me?'

'Are you kidding?' Ivy rolled her eyes as she sat back in her chair. 'You're sitting next to the girl who made "Famelia" happen!'

Maxie just blinked at her. Ivy remembered that Maxie did not go to Franklin Grove High, and so had no idea about the unlikely skater-boy and Goth-Queen match that Olivia had made.

'Never mind,' she said, grinning at the glee on

her sister's face as Olivia leaned forwards to start making plans.

Leave it to my twin, she thought. *The one person in the world with the power to turn a vampire crisis into a sweet love story!*

Half an hour later, Olivia led the whole group into One Planet, buzzing with happy anticipation. *This isn't just a successful mystery investigation, it's a true romance!*

Next to her, Ivy's leather jacket was zipped up all the way to her chin to conceal the stolen pashmina, which Maxie had handed over with obvious relief. Ivy was only wearing the pashmina until the twins and Reiko could take it back to the museum – but that wouldn't be until Stage Two of Operation: Maxie-Matchmaking had taken place!

As she pushed open the door to One Planet and heard the bell jingle over her head, Olivia had to stop herself from bouncing excitedly.

This couldn't be more perfect, she thought.

Artistic Maxie was just the right match for sweet, goth-no-more fashion designer Penny . . . and he liked her *so* much. He told them that his regular trips to One Planet were in the hope of running into Penny. The health food store was close to the art class she took on Wednesdays, and Penny just *loved* the gotu kola they sold. Maxie had gone there every week, hoping that he would one day work up the courage to talk to her.

He didn't even like gotu kola that much!

How adorable is that? Olivia beamed at her sister, who only replied with a rueful head-shake. Olivia knew that Ivy was desperate to return the pashmina to the museum without any more delays, but some things were too important to put off. Poor Maxie had clearly had a terrible week after his accidental theft. Even impatient Ivy had

understood that he needed help from them now
. . . even if she *still* didn't seem to truly understand
the importance of true love conquering all.
Olivia was determined to help Penny and Maxie
turn into . . . *Hmm. Pexie? Menny? Maxenny?*

OK, making up *their* couple-name was going
to take some time, even for her!

The bell over the door jingled, and Olivia spun
around, waving. 'Penny!'

'There you guys are!' Penny hurried towards
them, smiling. She was wearing a soft-looking
cornflower-blue top over a black skirt cut in such
a swirling pattern, Olivia was certain that Penny
must have designed it herself. 'Thanks so much
for inviting me to join you here. Has there been
any news about –?'

'Shh.' Olivia held one finger to her lips,
indicating the crowd of customers around them
. . . including Maxie, who stood in front of her,
slightly separate from their group, as if he had

not arrived with them. 'It's all been solved,' she whispered to Penny.

'Whew.' Penny let out a sigh of relief. 'I can't wait to tell Amelia.' She reached into her sunny yellow purse to pull out her cell phone.

'Wait!' Olivia grabbed her arm. 'Don't get on the phone now!'

Penny paused, looking confused. 'Why not?'

'Um . . . Because . . .' *Because it'll ruin my plan!*

Olivia started to panic. As soon as the line started moving again, Maxie was supposed to step aside and offer to let the girls all go ahead of them, because they were such a big group. *And that will get him and Penny talking!*

She couldn't tell that to Penny, though. 'Um . . .' Olivia flashed a desperate, *Help-me* look at Ivy. 'Because . . . because . . .'

Ivy answered as casually as if the whole fate of "Pexie" didn't rest on that moment. 'You should wait until we've gotten our drinks. There's terrible cell phone reception up here by the counter.'

'Oh. OK.' Penny dropped the phone back into her purse. 'Hmm, I wonder if I should go for the double shot of gotu kola?'

While Reiko and Penny launched into an enthusiastic discussion of health drinks, Olivia peered over the heads of the people in front of her. *Isn't this line ever going to move?* If their plan didn't get started soon, shy Maxie was almost certainly going to lose his nerve!

She popped up on to her toes . . . and groaned. *Oh, no.* Norah the server wasn't even bothering to make any drinks right now. She was much too busy leaning over the counter, flirting with Tall Tony, the comic book store owner!

Drat. So much for fixing him up with Blue Skye!

Olivia sighed. The truth was, she would actually think the scene in front of her was sweet, if only it weren't for the fact that this line *just wasn't moving.*

In front of her, Maxie shifted from foot to foot, plucking nervously at the cuffs of his shirt. As she watched, his eyes darted towards the door.

No! She tried to beam the silent message at him with pure willpower. *Do not turn tail and run. Not now!*

But oh, no . . . when she looked back at the front of the line, the flirtation had only grown more intense. Was Norah . . .? Oh, drat, she *was* — she was *twirling . . . her . . . hair!*

This is a disaster. Olivia clenched her fingers around her sparkly purple purse, desperately trying to think fast. *Time to come up with a Plan B!* But how could she get Penny and Maxie talking now? *Unless . . .*

'Reiko!' She spun around to face the exchange student.

'Huh?' Reiko broke off from her raving about the wonders of gotu kola. 'Did you say something?'

'Yes.' Olivia smiled purposefully as she looked at the tennis racquet still sticking dangerously out of Reiko's neon backpack. 'Can I borrow a comic book from you? Right now?'

The other three girls stared at her.

Ivy blinked. 'Um, Olivia? You want to start reading comics *now*?'

Olivia narrowed her eyes warningly at her twin. 'Well, I need something to read if we're going to be standing around for so long, right?'

'OK,' Reiko said. She shrugged, reaching for her backpack. 'I've got a couple in here.'

'Perfect,' Olivia said. *And here . . . we . . . go!*

She held her breath as Reiko un-shouldered her heavy backpack. Just as Olivia had hoped, the tennis racquet's handle arced around like a dangerous weapon.

'Ooh!' Penny leaped back just in time, just before she could get bopped on the head . . .

. . . And she bumped right into Maxie,

203

knocking his bag off his shoulder and on to the ground.

'I'm so sorry!' Penny gasped. 'I – oh. *Maxie!*' Pink flooded her cheeks. 'I . . . I didn't mean to . . .' Her cheeks flushed even pinker. Barely audibly, she mumbled, 'Um, how are you? You're not normally here unless it's a Wednesday. Um, I mean, not that I *notice* what days you're here or not . . . or anything. Ha-ha . . .'

Ignoring the chaos at his feet, Maxie gazed at Penny with big, adoring eyes. 'I – I – um, I mean, I'm fine. I'm . . . and you?'

Olivia gave a silent cheer of triumph. *They're talking . . . OK, they're barely getting their words out, but they're* trying!

Penny leaned towards Maxie, but she couldn't seem to bring herself to look back at him. 'I'm . . . fine,' she said softly. 'Just fine. How are you?'

Awww! Olivia clasped her hands together in delight as she turned to Ivy and Reiko.

A wide grin stretched Reiko's face under her pink-and-black hair. Ivy was smiling even as she shook her head and mimed bowing down to her twin.

'*You win again,*' Ivy mouthed silently.

Olivia sighed happily. It looked like Maxie wasn't the only one who had a crush . . . and "Menny" was well on its way to becoming Olivia's latest – and cutest – matchmaking triumph!

Why can't all romances be this simple?

Olivia would have loved to watch the scene unfold . . . but Ivy was already moving forwards to grab her arm and whisper in her ear.

'These two won't even notice if we take off.' Ivy gave an impatient jerk of her shoulders. 'I *need* to get this pashmina into the museum before anything else can go wrong. Every second I wait, it starts to feel even heavier. Seriously, it's already feeling like twenty pounds!'

'OK.' With one last, triumphant smile, Olivia

sidled away from 'Paxie' and towards the door.

As the doorbell jingled over their heads, the three girls exploded on to the street.

'Score!' Reiko carolled. She bounced an invisible basketball in her hands and made a perfect, invisible shot into an imaginary hoop. 'We did it!'

'Everything's working out perfectly,' Olivia cheered. 'All we have to do now is get the pashmina back into the museum, and then –'

She was interrupted by Ivy's phone ringing. Ivy took it out of her jacket pocket. 'Huh. It's Dad. We'd better both take this one.' Frowning, she put the phone on loudspeaker mode as she held it out between her and Olivia. 'Hello?'

'Is your sister with you?' Charles sounded worried. 'I think both of you should head to the museum as soon as possible . . . I just hope you won't be too late.'

Olivia gasped, crowding close to Ivy. 'What's

wrong?' she asked, even though she was kind of afraid of the answer. *Has someone discovered that the pashmina is a fake?*

'Alex and Tessa are just about to stop by to say farewell before they leave.'

'What?' Ivy's voice came out as a near-shout. 'But they weren't supposed to go home for at least another week!'

'I know.' Charles's sigh gusted through the phone line. 'Unfortunately, they've decided to cut their trip short.'

'But why?' Ivy looked ready to tear her hair out, and Olivia knew exactly why.

They can't leave now! Not before we've replaced the pashmina!

Charles's tone was heavy. 'You won't believe what's happened to them now.'

Oh, no. Olivia closed her eyes.

The phone signal flickered, cutting off most of Charles's words, but the few that Olivia caught were more than enough to convey the horror story.

'. . . garlic . . . fang . . . contact lens!'

'*Ouch.*' Ivy and Reiko both spoke at once, cringing.

'And they're coming to the *museum* to say goodbye?' Olivia whispered. Then she winced. *Of course they are.*

They would definitely want to pick up their 'lucky' pashmina before they left.

The twins couldn't let them carry the replica all the way back to Transylvania!

Ivy's face hardened with determination. 'We'll be there as soon as we can.' She snapped the phone shut.

Olivia, Reiko and Ivy all shared one frantic look as they absorbed the news.

Then, without a word, they turned and ran. The two vampires shot ahead within moments. Olivia struggled behind, panting. She didn't ask them to slow down, though, even as they turned the corner well ahead of her and disappeared.

We don't have any time to waste!

Chapter Eleven

Twenty-three minutes later, Ivy led the charge on to the museum's front steps, with Olivia gasping at the back. *Poor Olivia,* Ivy thought. Without a vampire's strength or speed, her twin had still run flat-out, first to the bus from Lincoln Vale, and then from the bus stop to the museum – all while wearing kitten-heels!

I have to buy her some tennis shoes for our next adventure, Ivy decided. For now, though, she just lunged towards the front door.

'Wait!' Olivia panted, leaning over with her hands on her knees and her usually smooth brown hair sticking to her face as she inclined her head towards the street nearby. 'Look. They're here.'

Whew. Ivy let out her breath as she saw the unmistakable royal figures of Alex and Tessa walking down the street towards them.

Now, where's Brendan? She scanned the long street but didn't see any sign of her boyfriend. *Oh, no!* She'd texted him to meet them at the museum, specifically so that he could distract Prince Alex while Olivia distracted Tessa, Reiko distracted Charles, and Ivy replaced the pashmina.

When did a simple 'switch' become so complicated? How are we going to do this without him?

'Hello!' Prince Alex's voice boomed down the street. He raised one hand, looking weary, but pleased to see them. 'I'm so glad you made it.'

'Thank darkness.' Tessa gave a weak smile as she walked with him towards the steps. 'I was so worried we wouldn't be able to say goodbye before we left.'

'We'd *never* let that happen.' Ivy tried to smile back, but her hands were sweating so much, it was hard to concentrate. *I just hope no one tries to give me a hug!* There was no way that Alex or Tessa would miss the feel of the pashmina bulking under her jacket . . . To Ivy, it was feeling like it weighed at least fifty pounds!

Act normal, she ordered herself. She started forwards – then stepped back. *Wait. What* is *'normal'? I don't even know any more!*

'Do you really have to leave so soon?' Olivia asked. 'It's a pity to only see you for such a short time!'

'I know.' Tessa sighed as she joined them on the steps. 'I'm disappointed, too, but it's been a long and . . . well, a rather difficult few days. Also . . .' She touched her baseball cap with a pained smile. 'I need to get back to my stylist in Transylvania to sort out the mess that is my hair!'

Alex rubbed her shoulder comfortingly. 'I'm

sure she'll fix it beautifully,' he told her. He sighed as he turned back to the twins and Reiko. 'My mother has a few "important" functions planned for next week, so Tessa and I really need to look our best. If only the myths were real, and vampires couldn't show up in photos!'

'Ha!' Ivy grinned. 'That's exactly what I thought just before the fashion show at Café Creative!'

Alex and Tessa both laughed sympathetically.

'But you looked beautiful at the show,' Tessa said. 'Truly. Even wearing Olivia's dress!'

'Well . . .' Ivy gulped. Suddenly, the pashmina she was wearing – *Tessa's* pashmina – felt like it was a living thing, crawling and tightening around her shoulders. How was she going to get it back in place without them noticing?

She couldn't tell them what had happened, not without getting poor Maxie into serious trouble. But otherwise . . .

'Do you want to go for a quick smoothie first, before we go inside?' she blurted.

'Ugh!' Tessa shuddered and stepped back. 'I'm sorry, but I don't ever want to go to Mister Smoothie's again! Not after last time.'

'Never,' Alex agreed. He put one hand to his head as if testing it for leftover drops of peach juice.

'Besides,' Tessa added, 'I've been so longing to really *see* the museum. I've been hoping that your father might even give us a quick tour of his triumphant Transylvanian exhibit before we head off. We can see the pashmina in its place of honour, and then I'm afraid we will take it back home. I'm just too nervous to be without it any more.'

'Well, then . . .' Olivia's smile was bright, but Ivy could clearly see the panic behind it. 'I can't think of a single reason to refuse that request. Not one. Who could?' Her voice rose, growing tight with panic. 'Ivy? Reiko? There's no way we can say "no". Right? I mean, who could possibly think of a reason to say "no" to that? There is no reason!'

Uh-oh. Olivia's about to lose it!

Ivy grabbed her twin's hand and pulled Olivia with her to the front door. 'You're absolutely right,' she said. 'There's no reason to refuse the request. So let's give Alex and Tessa that tour . . . and make sure it's *memorable*!'

'OK?' Olivia whispered.

As Ivy pushed the front door open, she felt her sister's gaze focus on her in a silent message: *Are you sure you know what you're doing?*

Ivy stepped inside to hold the door open for the rest of the group, giving her twin the most confident smile she could manage.

Let's just hope she doesn't guess . . . that I don't have a single clue what I'm going to do now!

'Are you all right?' Alex looked at Olivia with

concern as they walked inside. 'You seem a little breathless.'

'Oh . . .' Olivia gave him a weak smile, still panting from her earlier exertion. 'I'm just really excited about getting back into the museum, that's all.'

'Wow!' Alex's eyes widened. 'Now I'm *really* looking forward to this tour!'

Uh-oh. A nervous shiver ran all the way down Ivy's spine. *Whatever it is that I'm about to do . . . it has to work!*

Reiko was the last inside, looking around with bright curiosity.

Darting around the others, Ivy caught Reiko's eye and mouthed: '*Stall them!*'

Then she ran, leaving Reiko and Olivia to make her excuses.

Ivy's feet pounded on the marble floors of the museum, sending crashing echoes through the long display rooms and making museum guests

216

turn and stare as she passed. She couldn't stop, or even slow down. She just had to get to the decoy pashmina before –

'Ivy!' Strong hands grabbed her shoulders. 'Watch out! You were about to crash into me.'

'Dad!' Ivy fell back, panting, as Charles looked down at her with a concerned expression.

Oh, no. The last thing she needed right now was for her dad to see her . . . *no, wait. Maybe this is the perfect solution after all!*

'I was just trying to find you,' Ivy said. She forced a smile, pushing her hair out of her eyes. 'Alex and Tessa are here, and they really want an impromptu tour of your exhibit . . . but Olivia and I think you should show them around somewhere else first.'

'Sorry?' Charles blinked. 'What do you mean?'

'To whet their interest,' Ivy improvised. 'You know, to build up the excitement and make them even more eager for the main attraction!' *I need some Olivia-style filmspeak now!* Her twin would have come up with some grand Hollywood kind of explanation. All Ivy could think of right now, though, was . . . 'Please?'

'Well, of course I will!' Beaming, Charles rubbed his hands together. 'Oh my darkness. Personally invited to give a private tour to the prince and princess . . . how could I possibly resist?'

'Perfect.' Ivy slumped with relief. 'And you'll really take your time with it? No rushing?'

Charles shook his head at her reprovingly. 'What do you take me for, Ivy? A museum is to be *savoured*, not skipped through! Now, just let me think. Where is the perfect place to start?'

Mumbling to himself, he brushed past her. A minute later, she heard the sound of his booming voice echoing through the halls: 'Prince Alex, Princess Tessa! Let me introduce you to our museum.'

Whew. Ivy hurried forward into the costume room of the Transylvanian exhibit. Luckily, it was empty at the moment, as the other museum visitors still worked their way through the rooms closer to the front door.

Unzipping her leather jacket, she weaved her way around the glass cases, past richly-coloured medieval gowns and cloaks. The deep red glow of Penny and Amelia's replica pashmina shone like a beacon in the soft lights of the museum, calling her towards it.

Pulling off the real pashmina, Ivy let out her breath in a whoosh of relief. The weight was finally off her shoulders!

But this has to go absolutely perfectly!

Her hands shook with tension as she opened the glass door of the pashmina's display case. As carefully as she could, she lifted the replica pashmina off its velvet hanger with her left hand, while she held the real pashmina ready in her right.

It's almost over . . .

'Boo!'

Ivy leaped a full foot in the air, spinning around.

Brendan stood in the doorway, grinning goofily as he made a mock-bow. 'Sorry I'm late – but did it actually work? Did I really startle the ever-cool Ivy Vega?'

'Brendan!' Ivy grabbed the ends of her hair. She had to tug at it hard to stop herself from breaking down and crying. 'How could you do that to me?!'

'Sorry?' His grin faded. 'I just wanted to make you laugh. Was it bad timing?'

'*Bad timing?*' Ivy repeated incredulously. She pointed one shaking finger at the display case in front of her. 'Just look!'

The velvet hanger hung empty in the display case, while two deep red pashminas lay tangled on the floor – exactly where she'd dropped them at the sound of his voice.

'How am I supposed to tell which is the real one now?' she whispered.

'Oh, no.' Brendan's jaw dropped open. Then he glanced back over his shoulder, and turned even paler than usual. 'Your dad's on his way – with Alex and Tessa!'

Ivy dropped to her knees, desperately trying to untangle the two pashminas. Both of them were the same rich red . . . Both of them had *exactly* the same patterns. 'Can *you* tell which is which?' she asked hopelessly.

Brendan knelt down beside her. He shook his head, dark hair flopping over his brow. 'I didn't even look all that closely at the real one.'

'And now it's too late.' Ivy let out a growl of frustration. 'Penny and Amelia did *too* good a job with their replica. It's absolutely perfect . . . which is exactly what we *don't* need right now!'

Brendan asked tentatively, 'Could you make a guess?'

'You mean, just give Alex and Tessa the one that I *hope* is real?' Ivy swallowed hard, considering it. If the superstition really was all in the couple's minds, then they'd certainly feel better and more optimistic the moment they had *a* pashmina in their hands, no matter which one it really was . . . but . . .

Nope. Ivy's shoulders sagged as she accepted the truth. The series of bad luck that Alex and Tessa had had on their trip was definitely not just 'in their minds'. Even Ivy was starting to believe there was something spooky going on, and – considering the nightmares they'd already gone through – she couldn't bear to imagine what *new* horrors might befall the royal couple if they actually took home a *fake* Vein of Love!

'Hey, wait a minute.' Frowning, Brendan bent over one of the pashminas. 'What's that in the corner?'

'Where?' Ivy peered over his shoulder . . . and let out a disbelieving laugh. 'Thank darkness!'

The letters *AT* and *PT* were embroidered in such tiny letters that only vampire vision could have spotted them easily . . . but they were exactly the clue that Ivy needed.

Amelia Thompson and Penny Taylor! The two designers hadn't been able to resist leaving their mark on the fabric, and Ivy could have hugged them both for it.

'There!' She let out a whooshing sigh of relief and straightened, holding both of the pashminas in her hands . . .

. . . Just as a gasp sounded behind her. 'Ivy?' Tessa said. 'What exactly are you doing?'

Oh, no! Ivy turned around slowly. The royal

couple and her father were staring at her open-mouthed . . . and at the two identical pashminas in her arms.

Behind them, Olivia and Reiko hovered, looking panicked.

Think fast, Vega!

'Hey!' Pasting a smile on to her face, she waved the replica pashmina at Tessa. 'Isn't this cool? It's the replica we're going to put on display here after the real one is taken back to Transylvania.'

Charles blinked. 'It *is*?'

'Penny and Amelia just finished it,' Ivy said. 'I didn't want to tell you guys until I was absolutely sure it would work. I was just holding both pashminas now because . . . because . . .'

'To show Tessa!' Reiko finished for her. She bounded forwards as if she were about to play a round of tennis. 'Ivy said she wanted to get them both ready for Tessa to see before she left. To make sure the replica passes the test!'

'Yes!' Ivy said, relaxing. 'That's it!'

'My darkness.' Shaking her head in wonder, Tessa stepped forwards. 'Well, then. Shall I take a look?'

'Yes, please.' Ivy passed the decoy pashmina to the princess, aiming a grateful look at Reiko along the way.

The exchange student had provided the perfect explanation – and better yet, it wouldn't even be a real lie if only Charles agreed to put the replica on permanent display. After all, who could possibly be better at checking its accuracy than Tessa?

Prince Alex moved behind Tessa to take a look, as the princess stroked one finger gently across the replica.

'I can't believe it,' Tessa murmured. 'If I didn't know my pashmina so well, even I would never have guessed this was a copy!' She didn't seem to be able to look away as she turned the decoy pashmina over in her hands. 'Whoever made this did an incredible job!'

Yes! Ivy shared a secret smile with her twin as the royal couple bent over the pashmina, exclaiming together over all the perfect details. She made a mental note to tell Amelia and Penny just how great their replacement really was!

'And this belongs to you,' Ivy said. The final knots of tension rolled out of her shoulders as she handed the real pashmina back to Tessa. 'Thank you so much for lending it to the museum.'

And thank darkness we were able to give it back undamaged! She could see Olivia and Reiko sharing relieved glances. Brendan shifted closer to her, giving her hand a discreet squeeze.

'Ivy saves the day again!' he whispered in her ear.

'Not on my own,' Ivy whispered back. She beamed at Olivia and Reiko – the perfect partners in detection.

'So, Reiko?' Prince Alex turned to the exchange student. 'How have you liked America so far?'

'Well . . .' Scooping a tennis ball out of her backpack, Reiko grinned and started juggling it in her hands. 'This first week hasn't been quite what I expected, but it's still been pretty fun.' She winked at Ivy. 'And now I'm looking forward to Week Two!'

Ivy grinned back at her new friend. 'So am I,' she said. 'Even if I do have to go to an actual sports game by the end of it!'

'Are you still dreading that?' Reiko tossed her the tennis ball and pumped her fist triumphantly as Ivy caught it. 'Come on. It can't be any harder to sit through a game than it was to walk through a whole fashion show, right?'

'Well . . .' Ivy sighed.

'I almost forgot!' Alex scooped his smart-phone out from his pocket. 'Have you all seen the latest one?'

Ivy frowned. 'The latest what?'

Brendan let out a snicker. 'Oh, I can't wait for this . . .'

Charles gave her a fond smile. 'Ivy, Ivy, Ivy. Do you even have to ask?'

'She hasn't had much time to go on the Vorld Vide Veb,' Reiko explained to the others.

'Oh, no.' Ivy groaned. 'You don't mean –'

'Of course we do.' Alex held out the phone, grinning. 'Take a look.'

It was *the* viral photo, yet again – Olivia-as-Ivy grinning out at the camera in her slinky goth dress.

But every vampire in the room laughed as they read the caption:

Woohoo – I am the happiest vampire in the world!!!

'Arrrgh.' Ivy clapped her free hand to her eyes. But as the laughter of her friends and family surrounded her, even she couldn't help a reluctant chuckle. 'OK, maybe it's a *little* bit funny,' she admitted. 'But –'

'Never mind.' Her father's hand landed comfortingly on her shoulder. 'Fashion disasters are just a natural part of growing up, aren't they?'

'I guess so,' Ivy mumbled. 'The only thing is . . . I never expected *my* fashion frightmare to actually be my twin's.'

'And you know what that means?' Brendan poked her in the arm. 'Yours is still to come.'

The other vampires all burst into laughter again. Still cringing, Ivy dropped her hand away from her eyes . . . and found Olivia giving her a rueful smile.

Ivy let out her breath. *What am I worried about?* She smiled back.

No matter how bad my own fashion frightmare may be, I know Olivia will help me face it.

And with her twin at her side, Ivy wasn't scared of anything. Not even the colour pink!

VAMP MAGAZiNE

Sunset Scribbles – Olivia's Diary

VAMP MAGAZiNE has the most fangtastic treat for our younger readers – an **exclusive** sneak peek at the on-set diary kept by our favourite bunny twin, Olivia Abbott, during the making of her upcoming movie, **Eternal Sunset.**

There is **huge** buzz about this big-budget adaptation of one of the most popular Count Vira novels. Olivia plays immortal vampire twin sisters in love with human twin brothers!

Of course, falling in love with the twin boys is easy when they're played by Jackson Caulfield! Read on to discover if Olivia sheds any light on the rumours that their romance was rekindled between takes!

❧ September ❧

OK, Lesson #1: making movies is tiring! But it's also fun. We're kicking things off in London, England. We're filming the Victorian-era scenes, which means I get to wear lots of gorgeous dresses . . . although I also have to wear corsets . . . *sadface* Seriously, how did Victorian ladies breathe?!

I've had a small film role before – in The Groves – but that has NOT prepared me for the pressures of a lead role. I have so much dialogue to learn – for two different characters – and there are occasionally lots of takes needed. (I think my record was 40!) Jackson NEVER stumbles over his lines – he must have a photographic memory. I hate him for being so lucky! Well, I don't hate him . . . Obviously!

London is a beautiful city and I'd love to take Ivy back there one day to show her all the cool old buildings. When we weren't filming, most of the cast would go sightseeing. Of course, I have an easier time with this than poor Jackson, who needs to adopt a disguise before he steps outside of his hotel. His favorite trick is to pose as a regular English soccer fan, with a baggy jersey and a loud cap pulled low over his face – but although Jackson does most things BRILLIANTLY, a Cockney accent is NOT one of them. (He's going to be so mad at me when he reads this – teehee!!!)

✦ ✦ ✦

We've finished up the Victorian London scenes, and are now in New York City for the 1950s sequences. Score one for the 1950s – these gorgeous dresses don't need corsets! Strike one against the 1950s – my hair is almost as tall as I am. It deserves its own trailer! It looks fabulous, though. (If I do say so myself!)

🦇 October 🦇

We're not scheduled for much filming this month, because the production crew is still building sets for scenes we will be shooting in a town called Pine Wood, in November. Jackson insists these kinds of delays are normal, and I'm actually quite relieved to spend more than a single week at my new High School. I miss my sister!

🦇 November 🦇

After taking almost all of October off, we're back into the swing of things and are almost done with shooting. We've just wrapped a sequence that takes place in sixteenth century Venice – except we didn't have to travel there. The production built three massive rooms on a soundstage for us to film in. Jackson was playing "old man" versions of his characters, and had to wear make-up and white wigs for days. He said it was OK, but I could tell he was uncomfortable. He didn't complain once, though – he's such a trooper!

It's late November, and we're off to Pine Wood, for our last block of shooting. I'm excited because Debi

Morgan, a girl from my middle school in Franklin Grove, recently moved there. It will be cool to see her again. I also hear that Winifred Peters, the writer of the books, will be stopping by to visit the production, which would be awesome – I'd love to meet her!

Sadface at the idea this will be the last time I see everybody, though. It's a really great group of people that I've come to know and love over the past few months. On the set of a movie, you are constantly with the same bunch of people. You are up at dawn with them; staying late on the set with them; sitting with them for hours as you wait for the weather to change, and then suddenly it's over and everybody goes home . . .

Movie-making is odd like that!

"Sunset Scribbles – Olivia's Diary" will be in stores next year. Eternal Sunset will also be released next year, and we **can't wait to buy our tickets!!!**

EGMONT PRESS: ETHICAL PUBLISHING

Egmont Press is about turning writers into successful authors and children into passionate readers – producing books that enrich and entertain. As a responsible children's publisher, we go even further, considering the world in which our consumers are growing up.

Safety First
Naturally, all of our books meet legal safety requirements. But we go further than this; every book with play value is tested to the highest standards – if it fails, it's back to the drawing-board.

Made Fairly
We are working to ensure that the workers involved in our supply chain – the people that make our books – are treated with fairness and respect.

Responsible Forestry
We are committed to ensuring all our papers come from environmentally and socially responsible forest sources.

**For more information, please visit our website at
www.egmont.co.uk/ethical**